The Borrowers Afield

Also by Mary Norton

THE BORROWERS
THE BORROWERS AFLOAT
THE BORROWERS ALOFT
THE BORROWERS AVENGED
BED-KNOB AND BROOMSTICK
POOR STAINLESS
ARE ALL THE GIANTS DEAD?

ODYSSEY CLASSIC

The Borrowers Afield

MARY NORTON

Illustrated by Beth and Joe Krush

An Odyssey Classic
Harcourt Brace & Company
San Diego   New York   London

Requests for permission to make copies
of any part of the work should be mailed to:
Permissions Department, Harcourt Brace & Company, 6277 Sea Harbor Drive,
Orlando, Florida 32887-6777.

Library of Congress Cataloging-in-Publication Data
Norton, Mary.
The Borrowers afield/Mary Norton.
p.   cm
Sequel: The Borrowers afloat.
"An Odyssey Classic."
Summary: The further adventures of the family of miniature people
who, after losing their home under the kitchen floor of an old
English house, are forced to move out to the fields.
ISBN 0-15-210166-7
ISBN 0-15-210535-2 pb
[1. Fantasy.]   I. Title.
[PZ7.N8248Bi   1990]
[Fic]—dc20   89-39891

Printed in the United States of America
I H G F E D

The Borrowers Afield

1

"What has been, may be."
First recorded eclipse of the moon, 721 B.C.

[Extract from Arrietty's Diary and
Proverb Book, March 19th]

It was Kate who, long after she was grown up, completed the story of the borrowers. She wrote it all out, many years later, for her four children, and compiled it as you compile a case history or a biographical novel from all kinds of evidence—things she remembered, things she had been told and one or two things, we had better confess it, at which she just guessed. The most remarkable piece of evidence was a miniature Victorian notebook with gilt-edged pages, discovered by Kate in a gamekeeper's cottage on the Studdington estate near Leighton Buzzard, Bedfordshire.

Old Tom Goodenough, the gamekeeper, had never wanted the story put in writing, but as he had been dead now for so many years and as Kate's children were so very much alive, she thought perhaps that wherever he might be (and with a name like Goodenough it was bound to be Heaven) he would have overcome this kind of prejudice and would by now, perhaps, forgive her and understand. Anyway, Kate, after some thought, decided to take the risk.

When Kate had been a child herself and was living with her parents in London, an old lady shared their home (she was, I think, some kind of relation): her name was Mrs. May. And it was Mrs. May, on those long winter evenings beside the fire when she was teaching Kate to crochet, who had first told Kate about the borrowers.

At the time, Kate never doubted their existence—a race of tiny creatures, as like to humans as makes no matter, who live their secret lives under the floors and behind the wainscots of certain quiet old houses. It was only later that she began to wonder (and how wrong she was she very soon found out: there were still to be, had she only known it, developments more unlooked for and extraordinary than any Mrs. May had dreamed of).

The original story had smacked a little of hearsay: Mrs. May admitted—in fact, had been at some pains to convince Kate—that she, Mrs. May, had never actually seen a borrower herself; any knowledge of such beings she had gained at second hand from her younger brother, who, she admitted, was a little boy with not only a vivid imagination but well known to be a tease. So there you were, Kate decided—thinking it over afterwards—you could take it or leave it.

And, truth to tell, in the year or so which followed she tended rather to leave it: the story of the borrowers became pushed away in the back of Kate's mind with other childish fantasies. During this year she changed her school, made new friends, acquired a dog, took up skating and learned to ride a bicycle. And there was no thought of borrowers in Kate's mind (nor did she notice the undercurrent of excitement in Mrs. May's usually calm voice) when, one morning at breakfast in early spring, Mrs. May passed a letter across the table, saying, "This will interest you, Kate, I think."

It didn't interest Kate a bit (she was about eleven years old at the time): she read it through twice in a bewildered kind of way but could make neither head nor tail of it. It was a lawyer's letter from a firm called Jobson, Thring, Beguid and Beguid. Not only was it full of long words like "beneficiary" and "disentailment" but even the medium-sized words were arranged in such a manner that, to Kate, they made no sense at all. (What for instance could "vacant possession" mean? However much you thought about it, it could only describe a state of affairs which was manifestly quite impossible.) Names there were in plenty—Studdington, Goodenough, Amberforce, Pocklinton—and quite a family of people who spelled their name "deceased" with a small "d."

"Thank you very much," Kate had said politely, passing it back.

"I thought, perhaps," said Mrs. May (and her cheeks, Kate noticed, seemed slightly flushed as though with shyness), "you might like to go down with me."

"Go down where?" asked Kate, in her vaguest manner.

"My dear Kate," exclaimed Mrs. May, "what was the point of showing you the letter? To Leighton Buzzard, of course."

Leighton Buzzard? Years afterwards, when Kate described this scene to her children, she would tell them how, at these words, her heart began to thump long before her mind took in their meaning. Leighton Buzzard . . . she knew the name, of course: the name of an English country town . . . somewhere in Bedfordshire, wasn't it?

"Where Great Aunt Sophy's house was," said Mrs. May, prompting her. "Where my brother used to say he saw the borrowers." And before Kate could get back her breath she went on, in a matter-of-fact voice, "I have been left a little cottage, part of the Studdington estate, and"—her color deepened as though what she was about to say now might sound slightly incredible—"three hundred and fifty-five pounds. Enough," she added, in happy wonderment, "to do it up."

Kate was silent. She stared at Mrs. May, her clasped hands pressed against her middle as though to still the beating of her heart.

"Could we see the house?" she said at last, a kind of croak in her voice.

"Of course, that's why we're going."

"I mean the big house, Aunt Sophy's house?"

"Oh, that house? Firbank Hall, it was called." Mrs. May seemed a little taken aback. "I don't know. We could ask, perhaps; it depends of course on whoever is living there now."

"I mean," Kate went on, with controlled eagerness, "even if we couldn't go inside, you could show me the grating, and Arrietty's bank; and even if they opened the front door only ever so little, you could show me where the clock was. You could kind of point with your finger, quickly—" And, as Mrs. May still seemed to hesitate, Kate added suddenly on a note of anguish, "You did believe in them, didn't you? Or was it"—her voice faltered—"only a story?"

"And what if it were only a story?" said Mrs. May quickly, "so long as it was a good story? Keep your sense of wonder, child, and don't be so literal. Anything we haven't experienced for ourselves sounds like a story. All we can ever do is sift the evidence."

Sift the evidence? There was, Kate realized, calming down a little, a fair amount of that. Even before Mrs. May had spoken of such creatures, Kate had suspected their existence. How else to explain the steady, but inexplicable, disappearance of certain small objects about the house?

Not only safety pins, needles, pencils, blotting paper, matchboxes and those sorts of things. But, even in Kate's short life, she had noticed that if you did not use a drawer for any length of time you would never find it quite as you had left it: something was always missing—your best handkerchief, your

only bodkin, your carnelian heart, your lucky six-
pence. "But I *know* I put it in this drawer"—how
often had she said these words herself, and how
often had she heard them said? As for attics—! "I
am absolutely certain," Kate's mother had wailed
only last week, on her knees before an open trunk
searching vainly for a pair of shoe buckles, "that I
put them in this box with the ostrich-fan. They were
wrapped in a piece of black wadding and I slipped
them here, just below the handle. . . ." And the
same thing with writing desks, sewing baskets, but-
ton-boxes. There was never as much tea next day
as you had seen in the caddy the evening before.
Nor rice, for that matter, nor lump sugar. Yes, Kate

decided, there was evidence, if only she knew how to sift it.

"I suppose," she remarked thoughtfully, as she began to fold up her napkin, "some houses are more apt to have them than others."

"Some houses," said Mrs. May, "do not have them at all. And according to my brother," she went on, "it's the tidier houses, oddly enough, which attract them most. Borrowers, he used to say, are nervous people; they must know where things are kept and what each human being is likely to be doing at any hour of the day. In untidy, noisy, badly run houses, oddly enough, you can leave your belongings about with impunity—as far as borrowers are concerned, I mean." And she gave a short laugh.

"Could borrowers live out of doors?" asked Kate suddenly.

"Not easily, no," said Mrs. May. "They need human beings; they live by the same things human beings live by."

"I was thinking," went on Kate, "about Pod and Homily and little Arrietty. I mean—when they were smoked out from under the floor, how do you think they managed?"

"I often wonder," said Mrs. May.

"Do you think," asked Kate, "that Arrietty did

become the last living borrower? Like your brother said she would?"

"Yes, he said that, didn't he—the last of her race? I sincerely hope not. It was unkind of him," Mrs. May added reflectively.

"I wonder, though, how they got across those fields? Do you think they ever did find the badger's set?"

"We can't tell. I told you about the pillow case incident—when I took all the dollhouse furniture up there in a pillow case?"

"And you smelled something cooking? But that doesn't say our family ever got there—Pod and Homily and Arrietty. The cousins lived in the badger's set, too, didn't they—the Hendrearys? It might have been their cooking."

"It might, of course," said Mrs. May.

Kate was silent awhile, lost in reflection; suddenly her whole face lit up and she swiveled round in her chair.

"If we do go—" she cried (and there was an awed look in her eyes as though vouchsafed by some glorious vision), "where shall we stay? In an INN?"

2

"Without pains, no gains."
British Residency at Manipur attacked, 1891

[Extract from Arrietty's Diary and
Proverb Book, March 24th]

But nothing turns out in fact as you have pictured
it; the "inn" was a case in point—and so, alas, was
Great Aunt Sophy's house. Neither of these, to Kate,
were at all as they should be.

An inn, of course, was a place you came to at
night (not at three o'clock in the afternoon), pref-
erably a rainy night—wind, too, if it could be managed; and it should be situated on a moor ("bleak,"
Kate knew, was the adjective here). And there should
be scullions; mine host should be gravy-stained and
broad in the beam with a tousled apron pulled across
his stomach; and there should be a tall, dark
stranger—the one who speaks to nobody—warming
thin hands before the fire. And the fire should *be* a
fire—crackling and blazing, laid with an impossible
size log and roaring its great heart out up the chimney. And there should be some sort of cauldron,

Kate felt, somewhere about—and, perhaps, a couple of mastiffs thrown in for good measure.

But here were none of these things: there was a quiet-voiced young woman in a white blouse who signed them in at the desk; there was a waitress called Maureen (blond) and one called Margaret (mousy, with pebble glasses) and an elderly waiter, the back part of whose hair did not at all match the front; the fire was not made out of logs but of bored-looking coals tirelessly licked by an abject electric flicker; and (worst of all) standing in front of it, instead of a tall, dark stranger, was Mr. Beguid, the lawyer (pronounced "Be good")—plump, pink but curiously cool-looking, with silvery hair and a steel-gray eye.

But outside Kate saw the bright spring sunshine and she liked her bedroom with its view over the marketplace, its tall mahogany wardrobe and its constant hot and cold water coming from taps marked H and C. And she knew that tomorrow they would see the house—this legendary, mysterious house which now so surprisingly had become real, built no longer of airy fantasy but, she gathered, of solid bricks and mortar, standing firmly in its own grounds two miles along the road. Close enough, Kate realized, if only Mrs. May had not talked so much with Mr. Beguid, for them to have walked there after tea.

But when, next morning, they did walk there (Mrs. May in her long, slightly deerstalker-looking coat and with her rubber-tipped walking stick made of cherry wood), Kate was disappointed. The house looked nothing at all like she had imagined it. A barrack of red brick, it appeared to her, with rows of shining windows staring blankly through her, as though they were blind.

"They've taken the creeper down," said Mrs. May (she too sounded a little surprised), but after a moment, as they stood there at the head of the drive, she rallied slightly and added on a brisker note, "And quite right, too—there's nothing like creeper for damaging brickwork," and, as they began to walk on down the driveway, she went on to explain to Kate that this house had always been considered a particularly pure example of early Georgian architecture.

"Was it really *here*?" Kate kept asking in an incredulous voice as though Mrs. May might have forgotten.

"Of course, my dear, don't be so silly. This is where the apple tree was, the russet apple by the gate . . . and the third window on the left, the one with bars across, used to be my bedroom the last few times I slept here. The night-nursery of course looks out over the back. And there's the kitchen garden. We used to jump off that wall, my brother and I, and on to the compost heap. Ten feet high, it's supposed to be—I remember one day Crampfurl scolding us and measuring it with his besom."

(Crampfurl? So there had been such a person. . . .)

The front door stood open (as it must have stood, Kate realized suddenly, years ago on that never-to-be-forgotten day for Arrietty when she first saw the "great outdoors") and the early spring sunshine poured across the newly whitened step, into the high dark hall beyond; it made a curtain of light through which it was hard to see. Beside the step, Kate noticed, was an iron shoe-scraper. Was this the one down which Arrietty had climbed? Her heart began to beat a little faster. "Where's the grating?" she whispered, as Mrs. May pulled the bell. They heard it jangle far off in the dim distance, miles away it seemed.

"The grating?" said Mrs. May, stepping backwards on the gravel path and looking along the house front. "There," she pointed out, with a slight nod—keeping her voice low. "It's been repaired, but it's the same one."

Kate wandered toward it: yes, there it was, the actual grating through which they had escaped—

Pod, Homily and little Arrietty; there was the greenish stain and a few bricks which looked newer than the others. It stood higher than she had imagined; they must have had a bit of a jump to get down. Going up to it, she stooped, trying to see inside; dank darkness, that was all. So this had been their home. . . .

"Kate!" called Mrs. May softly, from beside the doorstep (as Pod must have called that day to Arrietty, when she ran off down the path) and Kate, turning, saw suddenly a sight she recognized, something which at last was as she had imagined it— the primrose bank. Tender, blue-green blades among the faded winter grasses—sown, spattered, almost drenched, they seemed, with palest gold. And the azalea bush, Kate saw, had become a tree.

After a moment, Mrs. May called again and Kate came back to the front door. "We'd better ring again," she said, and once more they heard the ghostly jangle. "It rings near the kitchen," explained Mrs. May, in a whisper, "just beyond the green baize door."

At last they saw a figure through the sunbeams; it was a slatternly girl in a wet, sackcloth apron, her bare feet in rundown sandals.

"Yes?" she said, staring at them and frowning against the sun.

Mrs. May stiffened. "I wonder," she said, "if I could see the owner of the house?"

"You mean Mr. Dawsett-Poole?" said the girl, "or the headmaster?" She raised her forearm, shading her eyes, a wet floor cloth, dripping slightly, clasped in a grimy hand.

"Oh," exclaimed Mrs. May. "Is it a school?" Kate caught her breath—that, then, explained the barrack-y appearance.

"Well, it always has been, hasn't it?" said the girl.

"No," replied Mrs. May, "not always. When I was a child I used to stay here. Perhaps, then, I might speak to whoever is in charge?"

"There's only my mum," said the girl. "She's the caretaker. They're all away over Easter—the masters and that."

"Well, in that case," began Mrs. May uncertainly, "I mustn't trouble you—" and was preparing to turn away when Kate, standing her ground, addressed the girl: "Can't we just see inside the hall?"

"Help yourself," said the girl, looking mildly surprised and she retreated slightly into the shadows as though to make way. "It's okay by me."

They stepped through the veil of sunlight into a dimmer coolness. Kate looked about her: it was wide and high and paneled and there were the stairs "going up and up, world upon world," as Arrietty had described them. All the same, the hall was nothing like she had imagined it. The floor was covered with burnished, dark green linoleum; there was a sourish smell of soapy water and the clean smell of wax.

"There's a beautiful stone floor under this," said Mrs. May, touching the linoleum with her rubber-tipped walking stick.

The girl stared at them curiously; in a moment, as though bored, she turned away and disappeared into the shadowy passage beyond the staircase, scuffling a little in her downtrodden shoes.

Kate, about to comment, felt Mrs. May's hand on her arm. "Listen," said Mrs. May sharply; and Kate, holding her breath to complete the silence, heard a curious sound, a cross between a sigh and moan. Mrs. May smiled. "That's it—" she whispered, "the sound of the green baize door."

"And where was the clock?" asked Kate.

Mrs. May indicated a piece of wall, now studded with a row of coat pegs. "There; Pod's hole must have been just behind where that radiator is now. A radiator, they'd have liked that. . . ." She pointed to a door across the hall, now labeled, in neat white lettering, "Headmaster's Study." "That was the morning room," she said.

"Where the Overmantels lived? And Pod got the blotting paper?" Kate stared a moment and then, before Mrs. May could stop her, ran across and tried the door.

"No, Kate, you mustn't. Come back."

"It's locked," said Kate. "Could we just peep upstairs? I'd love to see the night-nursery. I could go terribly quietly. . . ."

"No, Kate, come along: we must go now. We've no business to be here at all," and Mrs. May walked firmly toward the door.

"Couldn't I just peep in the kitchen window?" begged Kate when they stood once again in the sunshine.

"No, Kate," said Mrs. May.

"Just to see where they lived? Where that hole was under the stove which Pod used as a chute— *please*."

"Quickly, then," said Mrs. May. She threw a nervous glance in each direction as Kate sped off along the path.

This, too, was a disappointment. Kate knew where the kitchen was because of the grating, and making blinkers of her cupped hands against the reflected sunshine, she pushed her face up close against the glass. Dimly the room came into view, but it was nothing like a kitchen: shelves of bottles, gleaming retorts, heavy benchlike tables, rows of Bunsen burners. The kitchen was now a lab.

And that was that. On the way home, Kate picked a very small bunch of dog-violets; there was veal and ham pie for luncheon, with salad; with the choice of plums and junket or baked jam-roll; and, after luncheon, Mr. Beguid arrived with car and chauffeur to take them to see the cottage.

At first Kate did not want to go; she had a secret plan of walking up to the field called Perkin's Beck and mooching about by herself, looking for badgers' sets. But when Mrs. May explained to her that the field was just behind the cottage, and by the time Mr. Beguid had stared long enough and pointedly enough out of the window with a bored, dry, if-this-were-my-child kind of expression on his face, Kate decided to go in the car after all, just to spite him. And it was a good thing (as she so often told her own children years afterwards) that she did: otherwise, she might never have talked to or (which was more important) made friends with—Thomas Good-enough.

"And about vacant possession," Mrs. May asked in
the car, "he really is going, this old man? I've forgotten his name——"

"Old Tom Goodenough? Yes, he's going all right;
we've got him an almshouse. Not," Mr. Beguid added,
with a short laugh, "that he deserves it."

"Why not?" asked Kate in her blunt way.

Mr. Beguid glanced at her, a little put out, as
though the dog had spoken. "Because," he said,
ignoring Kate and addressing Mrs. May, "he's a
tiresome old humbug, that's why." He laughed again,
his complacent, short laugh. "The biggest liar in
five counties—they call him down in the village."

The stone cottage stood in a field; it stood high,
its back to the woods; it had a derelict look, Kate
thought, as they toiled up the slope toward it, but
the thatch seemed good. Beside the front door stood
a water-butt leaking a little at the seams and green

with moss; there was slime on the brick path and a thin trickle of moisture which lost itself among the dock and thistles. Against the far end was a wooden outhouse on the walls of which Kate saw the skins of several small mammals nailed up to dry in the sun.

"I didn't realize it was quite so remote," panted Mrs. May, as Mr. Beguid knocked sharply on the blistered paint of the front door. She waved her rubber-tipped stick toward the sunken lane below the sloping field of meadow grass. "We'll have to make some kind of proper path up here."

Kate heard a shuffling movement within and Mr. Beguid, rapping again, called out impatiently, "Come on, old Tom. Open up."

There were footsteps and, as the door creaked open, Kate saw an old man—tall, thin, but curiously heavy about the shoulders. He carried his head sunk a little onto his chest, and inclined sideways; and when he smiled (as he did at once), this gave him a sly look. He had bright, dark, strangely luminous eyes which he fixed immediately on Kate.

"Well, Tom," said Mr. Beguid briskly, "how are you keeping? Better, I hope. Here is Mrs. May, the lady who owns your cottage. May we come in?"

"There's naught to hide," said the old man, backing slightly, to let them pass, but smiling only at Kate. It was, Kate thought, as though he could not see Mr. Beguid.

They filed past him into the principal room. It was bare-ish but neat enough, except for a pile of wood shavings on the stone floor and a stack of something Kate took to be kindling beside the window embrasure. A small fire smoldered in a blackened grate which seemed to be half oven.

"You've tidied up a bit, I see," said Mr. Beguid, looking about him. "Not that it matters much," he added, speaking aside to Mrs. May, but barely lowering his voice. "Before the builders come in, if I were you I'd get the whole place washed through and thoroughly fumigated."

"I think it looks lovely," cried Kate warmly, shocked by this want of manners, and Mrs. May hastened to agree with her, addressing a friendly look toward the old man.

But old Tom gave no sign of having noticed; quietly he stood, looking down at Kate, smiling his secret smile.

"The stairs are through here," said Mr. Beguid, leading the way to a farther door. "And here," they heard him say, "is the scullery." Mrs. May, about to follow, hesitated on the threshold. "Don't you want to come, Kate, and see round the cottage?"

Kate stood stolidly where she was; she threw a

quick glance at the old man, and back again to Mrs. May. "No, thanks," she said shortly. And as Mrs. May, a little surprised, followed Mr. Beguid into the scullery, Kate moved toward the pile of peeled sticks. There was a short silence.

"What are you making?" Kate asked at last, a little shyly. The old man came back from his dream. "Them?" he said in his soft voice. "Them's sprays— for thatching." He picked up a knife, tested the blade on his horny thumb and pulled up a lowish stool. He sat down. "Come you here," he said, "by me, and I'll show 'ee."

Kate drew up a chair beside him and watched him in silence as he split a length of hazel which at first she had taken for kindling. After a moment, he said softly, without looking up, "You don't want to take no notice of him."

"Mr. Beguid?" said Kate. "I don't. Be Good! It's a silly kind of name. Compared to yours, I mean," she added warmly. "Whatever you did wouldn't matter really with a name like Good Enough."

The old man half turned his head in a warning gesture toward the scullery. He listened a moment and then he said, "They're going upstairs," and Kate, listening, too, heard clumping footsteps on wooden treads. "You know how long I bin in this cottage?" the old man asked, his head still cocked

as though listening while the footsteps crossed and recrossed what must have been his bedroom. "Nigh on eighty years," he added after a moment. He took up a peeled sapling, grasping it firmly at either end.

"And now you've got to go?" said Kate, watching his hands as he took a firmer grip on the wood.

The old man laughed as though she had made a joke: he laughed quite silently, Kate noticed, shaking his head. "So they make out," he said in an amused voice, and with a twist of his two wrists he wrung the tough sapling as you wring out a wet cloth, and in the same movement doubled it back on itself. "But I bain't going," he added and he threw the bent stick on the pile.

"But they wouldn't want to turn you out," said Kate, "not if you don't want to go. At least," she added cautiously, "I don't think Mrs. May would."

"Her-r-r?" he said, rolling the "r's" and looking up at the ceiling. "She's hand in glove with him."

"She used to come and stay here," Kate told him, "when she was a child. Did you know? Down at the big house. Firbank, isn't it?"

"Aye," he said.

"Did you know her?" asked Kate curiously. "She used to be called Miss Ada?"

"I knew Miss Ada all right," said the old man, "and her aunty. *And* her brother—" He laughed again. "I knew the whole bang lot of 'em, come to that."

As he spoke, Kate had a strange feeling. It was as though she had heard these words before spoken by just such an old man as this and, she seemed to remember, it was in some such similar place—the sunlit window of a darkish cottage on a bright but cold spring day. She looked round wonderingly at the whitewashed walls—flaking a little they were, in a pattern she seemed to recognize; even the hollows and cracks of the worn brick floor also seemed curiously familiar—strange, because (of this she was certain) she had never been here before. She looked back at old Tom, getting up courage to go a step further. "Did you know Crampfurl?" she asked after a moment, and even before he answered she knew what he would say. "I knew Crampfurl all right," and the old man laughed again, nodding his grizzled head, and enjoying some secret joke.

"And Mrs. Driver, the cook?"

Here the joke became almost too much for old Tom. "Aye," he said, wheezing with silent laughter. "Mrs. Driver!" and he wiped the corner of his eye with his sleeve.

"Did you know Rosa Pickhatchet," went on Kate, "that housemaid, the one who screamed?"

"Nay," said old Tom, nodding and laughing.

"But I heard tell of her—screamed the house down, so they say. . . ."

"But you know why?" cried Kate excitedly.

He shook his head. "No reason at all, as I can see."

"But didn't they tell you that she saw a little man, on the drawing room mantelshelf, about the size of the china cupid; that she thought he was an ornament and tried to dust him with a feather duster—and suddenly he sneezed? Anyone would scream," Kate concluded breathlessly.

"For why?" said old Tom, deftly sliding the bark from the wood as though it were a glove finger. "They don't hurt you, borrowers don't. And they don't make no mess neither. Not like field mice. Beats me, always has, the fuss folk'll make about a borrower, screeching and screaming and all that caper." He ran an appreciative finger along the peeled surface. "Smoking 'em out and them kind of games. No need for it, not with borrowers. They go quiet enough, give 'em time, once they know they've been seen. Now take field mice—" The old man broke off to twist his stick, catching his breath with the effort.

"Don't let's," cried Kate, "please! I mean, let's go on about borrowers—"

"There's naught to go on with," said the old man, tossing his stick on the pile and selecting a fresh one. "Borrowers is as like to humans as makes no matter, and what's to tell about humans? Now you take field mice—once one of them critturs finds a way indoors, you're done and strung up as you might say. You can't leave the place not for a couple of hours but you don't get the whole lot right down on you like a flock of starlings. Mess! And it ain't a question of getting 'em out. They've come and they've gone, if you see what I mean. Plague o' locusts ain't in it. Yes," he went on, "no doubt about it—in a house like this, you're apt to get more trouble from field mice than ever you get from any borrower. In a house like this," he repeated, "set away like at the edge of the woods, borrowers can be company, like as not." He glanced up at the ceiling which creaked slightly as footsteps passed and repassed in the room above. "What you reckon they're up to?" he said.

"Measuring," Kate said. "They'll be down soon," she went on hurriedly, "and I want to ask you something—something important. If they send me for a walk tomorrow—by myself, I mean, while they talk business—could I come up and be with you?"

"I don't see no reason why not," said the old man, at work on his next stick. "If you brings along a sharp knife, I'll learn you to make sprays."

"You know," went on Kate impressively, with a wary glance at the ceiling, "her brother, Mrs. May's brother—or Miss Ada's or whatever you like to call her—he *saw* those borrowers down at the big house!" She paused for effect, watching his face.

"What of it?" said the old man impassively. "You only got to keep your eyes skinned. I seen stranger things in my time than them sort of critturs. Take badgers—now you come up here tomorrow and I'll tell summat about badgers that you just wouldn't credit, but that I seen it with me own two eyes—"

"But have you ever seen a *borrower*?" cried Kate impatiently. "Did you ever see any of these ones down at the big house?"

"Them as they had in the stables?"

"No, the ones who lived under the kitchen."

"Oh, them," he said, "smoked out, they were. But it ain't true—" he went on, raising his face suddenly, and Kate saw that it was a sad face when it was not smiling.

"What isn't true?"

"What they say: that I set the ferret on 'em. I wouldn't. Not me. Not once I knew they was borrowers."

"Oh," exclaimed Kate, kneeling up on her chair with excitement. "You were the boy with the ferret?"

Old Tom looked back at her—his sideways look. "I were a boy," he admitted guardedly, "and I did have a ferret."

"But they did escape, didn't they?" Kate persisted anxiously. "Mrs. May says they escaped by the grating."

"That's right," said old Tom. "Made off across the gravel and up the bank."

"But you don't know for certain," said Kate, "you didn't see them go. Or could you see them from the window?"

"I knows for certain, all right," said old Tom. "True enough I saw 'em from the window, but that ain't how—" he hesitated, looking at Kate; amused he seemed but still wary.

"Please, tell me. Please—" begged Kate.

The old man glanced upward at the ceiling. "You know what he is?" he said, inclining his head.

"Mr. Beguid? A lawyer."

The old man nodded. "That's right. And you don't want nothing put down in writing."

"I don't understand," said Kate.

The old man sighed and took up his whittling knife. "What I tells *you*, you tells *her*, and *he* puts it all down in writing."

"Mrs. May wouldn't tell," said Kate. "She's—

"She's hand in glove with him, that's what I maintain. And it's no good telling me no different. Seemingly now, you can't die no more where you reckons to die. And you know for why?" he said, glaring at Kate. "Because of what's put down in writing." And with a curiously vicious twist he doubled the poor stick. Kate stared at him nonplused. "If I promised not to tell?" she said at last, in a timid voice.

"Promises!" exclaimed the old man; staring at Kate, he jerked a thumb toward the ceiling. "Her-r-r great uncle, old Sir Montague that was, promised me this cottage. 'It's for your lifetime, Tom,' he says. Promises!" he repeated angrily, and he almost spat the word. "Promises is piecrust."

Kate's eyes filled with tears. "All right," she said, "then don't tell me!"

Tom's expression changed, almost as violently. "Now don't 'ee cry, little maid," he begged, surprised and distressed.

But Kate, to her shame, could not stop; the tears ran down her cheeks and she felt the familiar hot feeling at the tip of her nose as though it was swelling. "I was only wondering," she gasped, fumbling for a handkerchief, "if they were all right . . . and how they managed . . . and whether they found the badger's set . . ."

"They found the badger's set all right," said old Tom. "Now, don't 'ee cry, my maiden, not no more."

"I'll stop in a minute," Kate assured him in a stifled voice, blowing her nose.

"Now look 'ee here," the old man went on— very upset he sounded. "You dry your eyes and stop your weeping and old Tom'll show you summat." Awkwardly he got up off his stool and hovered over her, drooping his shoulders like some great protective bird. "Something you'd like. How's that, eh?"

"It's all right," Kate said, giving a final scrub. She stuffed away her handkerchief and smiled up at him. "I've stopped."

Old Tom put his hand in his pocket and then, throwing a cautious glance toward the ceiling, he seemed to change his mind: for a moment it had sounded as though the footsteps had been moving toward the stairs. "It's all right," whispered Kate, after listening; and he fumbled again and drew out a battered tin box, the kind in which pipe smokers keep tobacco, and with his knotted fingers fumbled awkwardly with the lid. At last, it was open, and breathing heavily, he turned it over and slid something out. "There—" he said, and on his callused palm Kate saw the tiny book.

"Oh—" she breathed, staring incredulously.

"Take it up," said old Tom, "it won't bite you."

And, as gingerly Kate put out her hand, he added, smiling, " 'Tis Arrietty's diary."

But Kate knew this, even before she saw the faded gilt lettering, *Diary and Proverb Book*, and in spite of the fact that it was weather-stained and time-worn, that when she opened it the bulk of its pages slipped out from between the covers, and the ink or pencil or sap—or whatever Arrietty had used to write with—had faded to various shades of brown and sepia and a curious sickly yellow. It had opened at August the 31st, and the proverb, Kate saw, was "Better to suffer ill, than do ill," and below this the bald statement "Disastrous Earthquake at Charleston, U. S., 1866" and on the page itself, in Arrietty's

3 3

scratchy handwriting, were three entries for the three successive years:

Spiders in storeroom.

Mrs. D. dropped pan. Soup—leak in ceiling.

Talked to Spiller.

Who was Spiller, Kate wondered? August 31st? That was after they left the big house. Spiller, she realized, must be part of the new life, the life out-of-doors. At random, she turned back a few pages:

Mother bilious.

Threaded green beads.

Climbed hedge. Eggs bad.

Climbed hedge? Arrietty must have gone bird's-nesting—and the eggs would be bad in (Kate glanced at the date) . . . yes, it was still August, and the motto for that day was "Grasp all, lose all."

"Where did you get this book?" Kate asked aloud in a stunned voice.

"I found it," said old Tom.

"But where?" cried Kate.

"Here," said old Tom, and Kate saw his eyes stray in the direction of the fireplace.

"In this house," she exclaimed in an unbelieving voice and, staring up at his mysterious old face, Mr. Beguid's unkind words came back to her suddenly, "the biggest liar in five counties." But here, in her hand, was the actual book: she stared down at it, trying to sort out her thoughts.

"You want I should show you summat else?" he asked her, suddenly and a little pathetically, as though aware of her secret doubts. "Come you here," and getting up slowly from her chair, Kate followed like a sleepwalker as he went toward the fireplace.

Old Tom stooped down and, panting a little, he tugged at the heavy wood-box. As it shifted a board fell forward with a slight clatter and the old man, alarmed by the clatter, glanced at the ceiling; but Kate, leaning forward, saw the board had covered a sizable rat-hole gouged out of the skirting and gothic in shape, like an opened church door.

"See?" said old Tom, after listening a moment— a little breathless from tugging he sounded. "Goes right through to the scullery: they'd got fire this side and water t'other. Years, they lived here."

Kate knelt down, staring into the hole. "Here? In your house?" Her voice became more and more scared and unbelieving. "You mean . . . Pod? And Homily . . . and little Arrietty?"

"Them, too," said old Tom, "in the end, as it were."

"But didn't they live out-of-doors? That's what Arrietty was longing to do—"

"They lived out-of-doors all right"—he gave a short laugh—"if you can call it living. Or come to that, if you can call it outdoors! But you take a look at this," he went on softly with a note in his voice of thinly disguised pride, ". . . goes right up inside the wall, stairs they got and all betwixt the lath and the plaster. Proper tenement, they got here—six floors—and water on every floor. See that?" he asked, laying his hand on a rusty pipe. "Comes down from the cistern in the roof, that does, and goes on through to the scullery. Tapped it, they did, in six different places . . . and never a drop or a leak!"

He was silent a moment, lost in thought, before he propped back the board again and shoved the wood-box back into place. "Years they lived here," he said affectionately and he sighed a little as he straightened up, dusting his hands together.

"But *who* lived here?" Kate whispered hurriedly (the footsteps above had crossed the landing and were now heard approaching the head of the stairs). "You don't mean my ones? You said they found the badger's set."

"They found the badger's set all right," said old Tom, and gave his short laugh.

"But how do you know? Who told you?" Twittering with anxiety she followed behind him as he limped to his stool.

Old Tom sat down, selected a stick and, with maddening deliberation, tested the edge of his knife. "She told me," he said at last, and he cut the stick in three lengths.

"You mean you talked to Arrietty!"

He made a warning sign at her raised voice, lifting his eyebrows and jerking his head. The footsteps, Kate heard, were clumping now down the wooden treads of the stairs. "You don't talk to that one," he whispered, "not while she's got a tongue to wag."

Kate went on staring: if he had hit her on the head with a log from the log box, she could not have appeared more stunned. "Then she must have told you everything!" she gasped.

"Hush!" said the old man, his eye on the door. Mrs. May and Mr. Beguid, it seemed, had reached the bottom of the stairs, and from the sound of their voices had turned again into the scullery for a last look round. "Two fitted basins, at least," Mrs. May was heard saying, in a matter-of-fact tone.

"Pretty nigh on everything, I reckon," whispered old Tom. "She'd creep out most evenings, pretty regular." He smiled as he spoke, glancing toward the hearth. And Kate, watching his face, suddenly saw the picture: the firelit cottage, the lonely boy at his whittling and, almost invisible in the shadows

this tiny creature, seated maybe on a matchbox: the
fluty, monotonous voice going on and on and on . . .
after a while, Kate thought, he would hardly have
heard it: it would merge and become part of the
room's living stillness, like the simmer of the kettle
or the ticking of the clock. Night after night; week
after week; month after month; year, perhaps, after
year . . . Yes, Kate realized (staring in the same
stunned way even though, at this minute, Mrs. May
and Mr. Beguid came back to the room still talking
loudly of washbasins), Arrietty must indeed have
told Tom everything!

4

"No tale loses in the telling."
Longfellow, American Poet, died, 1882;
also Walt Whitman, 1892

[Extract from Arrietty's Diary and
Proverb Book, March 26th]

And all that was needed now, she thought (as she
lay that night in bed, listening to the constant gurgle
in the pipes of the constant H and C), was for old
Tom to tell *her* everything in as full detail—as Arrietty must have told it to him. And, having already
said so much, he might—she felt—go this much
farther, in spite of his fear of things put down in
writing. And she wouldn't tell either, she resolved
staunchly—at any rate, not during his lifetime, although why he should mind so much she couldn't
understand, seeing that he was known already as
"the biggest liar in five counties." But what seemed
still more hopeful was that, having shown her the
little book, he had not even asked for it back. She
had it now in bed with her, stuffed beneath her
pillow and it was full of "things in writing." Not that
she could understand them quite: the entries were
too short, little headings, they seemed like, jotted

down by Arrietty to remind herself of dates. But some of them sounded extraordinarily weird and mysterious . . . Yes, she decided, suddenly inspired, that was the way to work it: she would ask old Tom to explain the headings: what could Arrietty have meant (she would ask) by "Black men—mother saved."?

And this was, more or less, what did happen: while Mrs. May talked business each day with Messrs. Jobson, Thring, Beguid and Beguid, or argued with builders and plumbers and plumber's mates, Kate would wander off alone across the fields and find her own way to the cottage, seeking out old Tom.

On some days (as Kate, in later years, would explain to her children) he would seem a bit "cagey" and disinterested, but on other days a particular heading in the diary would seem to inspire him and his imagination would take wings and sail away on such swirls and eddies of vivid memory that Kate, spellbound, could hardly believe that he had not at some time (in some other life, perhaps) been a borrower himself. Mrs. May, Kate remembered, had said just this of her younger brother: this brother who, although three years his junior, must have known old Tom (Had not old Tom himself admitted this much?). Had they been friends—great friends, perhaps? They certainly seemed birds of a feather—

one famous for telling tall stories because "he was such a tease"; the other, more simply described as "the biggest liar in five counties." And it was this thought which, long after she was grown up, decided Kate to tell the world what was said to have happened to Pod and Homily and little Arrietty after that dreadful day when, smoked out of their house under the kitchen, they sought for refuge in the wild outdoors.

Here is her story—all "put down in writing." Let us sift the evidence ourselves.

5

"Step by step climbs The Hill."
Victoria Tubular Bridge, Montreal, opened, 1866

[Extract from Arrietty's Diary and
Proverb Book, August 25th]

Well, at first, it seems they just ran, but they ran
in the right direction—up the azalea bank, where
(so many months ago now) Arrietty had first met the
boy and through the long grass at the top. How they
got through that, Homily used to say afterwards, she
never knew—nothing but stalks, close set. And insects: Homily had never dreamed there could be so
many different kinds of insects—slow ones, hanging
on things; fast, scuttling ones, and ones (these were
the worst) which stared at you and did not move at
once and then backed slowly, still staring (it was as
though, Homily said, they had made up their mind
to bite you and then, still malicious, changed it out
of caution). "Wicked," she said, "that's what they
were; oh, wicked, wicked, wicked . . ."

As they shoved their way through the long grass,
they were choked with pollen loosened in clouds
from above; there were sharp-edged leaves, decep-

tively sappy and swaying, which cut their hands, gliding across the skin like the soft-drawn bow of a violin but leaving blood behind: there were straw-dry, knotted stems, which caught them round the shins and ankles and which made them stumble and trip forward; often they would land on that cushiony plant with silvery, hairlike spines—spines which pricked and stung. Long grass . . . long grass . . . forever afterward it was Homily's nightmare.

Then, to get to the orchard, came a scramble through the privet hedge: dead leaves, below the blackened boughs of privet . . . dead leaves and rotting, dried-up berries which rose waist-high as they swam their way through them, and, below the leaves, a rustling dampness. And here again were insects: things which turned over on their backs, or hopped suddenly, or slyly slid away.

Across the orchard—easier going this, because the hens had fed there achieving their usual "blasted heath" effect—a flattened surface of lava-colored earth: the visibility was excellent. But, if they could see, they could also be seen: the fruit trees were widely spaced, giving little cover: anyone glancing from a first-floor window in the house might well exclaim curiously, "What's that, do you think, moving across the orchard? There by the second tree on the right—like leaves blowing. But there isn't a wind. More like something being drawn along on a thread—too steady to be birds . . ." This was the thought in Pod's mind as he urged Homily onwards. "Oh, I can't," she would cry. "I must sit down. Just a moment, Pod—please!"

But he was adamant. "You can sit down," he'd say, gripping her below the elbow and spinning her forward across the rubble, "once we get to the spinney. You take her other arm, Arrietty, but keep her moving!"

Once within the wood, they sank down on the side of the well-worn path, too exhausted to seek further cover. "Oh, dear . . . oh, dear . . . oh, dear . . ." Homily kept saying (mechanically, because she always said it), but behind her bright dark eyes in her smudged face, they could see her brain was busy: and she was not hysterical, they could see that, too; they could see, in other words, that Homily was "trying." "There's no call for all this running," she said after a moment, when she could get her breath. "Nobody didn't see us go: fer all they know we're still there, trapped-like—under the floor."

"I wouldn't be so sure," said Arrietty. "There was a face at the kitchen window. I saw it as we were going up the bank. A boy it looked like, with a cat or something."

"If anyone'd seen us," remarked Homily, "they'd have been after us, that's what I say."

"That's a fact," said Pod.

"Well, which way do we go from here?" asked Homily, gazing about among the tree trunks. There was a long scratch across her cheek and her hair hung down in wisps.

"Well, we better be getting these loads sorted out first," said Pod. "Let's see what we've brought. What have you got in that borrowing-bag, Arrietty?"

Arrietty opened the bag she had packed so hurriedly two days before against just this emergency. She laid out the contents on the hardened mud of the path and they looked an odd collection. There were three tin lids off varying sizes of pill bottles which fitted neatly one inside the other; a sizable piece of candle and seven wax matches; a change of underclothes and an extra jersey knitted by Homily on blunted darning needles from a much-washed, unraveled sock, and last (but most treasured) her pencil from a dance program and her *Diary and Proverb Book*.

"Now why did you want to cart that along?" grumbled Pod, glancing sideways at this massive tome as he laid out his own belongings. For the same reason, Arrietty thought to herself as she glanced at Pod's unpacking, that you brought along your shoemaker's needle, your hammer made from an electric bell-clapper, and a stout ball of twine: each to his hobby and the tools of the craft he loves (and hers she felt to be literature).

Besides his shoemaking equipment, Pod had brought the half nail scissor, a thin sliver of razor blade, ditto of child's fretsaw, an aspirin bottle with screw lid filled with water, a small twist of fuse wire and two steel hat pins, the shorter of which he gave to Homily. "It'll help you up the hill," he told her. "We may have a bit of a climb."

Homily had brought her knitting needles, the rest of the raveled sock, three pieces of lump sugar, the finger of a lady's kid glove filled with salt and pepper mixed, tied up at the neck with cotton, some broken pieces of digestive biscuit, a small tin box made for phonograph needles which now contained dry tea, a chip of soap and her hair curlers.

Pod gazed glumly at the curious collection. "Like as not we brought the wrong things," he said, "but it can't be helped now. Better pack 'em up again," he went on, suiting the action to the word, "and let's get going. Good idea of yours, Arrietty, the way you fitted together them tin lids. Not sure, though, we couldn't have done with a couple more . . ."

"We've only got to get to the badger's set," Ar-

rietty excused herself. "I mean Aunt Lupy will have most things, won't she—like cooking utensils and such?"

"I don't know anyone as couldn't do with a few more," remarked Homily, stuffing in the remains of the sock and lashing up the neck of her bag with a length of blue embroidery silk, "especially when they live in a badger's set. And who's to say your Aunt Lupy's there at all?" she went on. "I thought she got lost or something, crossing them fields out walking."

"Well, she may be found again by now," said Pod. "Over a year ago, wasn't it, when she set out walking?"

"And anyway," Arrietty pointed out, "she wouldn't go walking with the cooking pots."

"I never could see," said Homily, standing up and trying out the weight of her bag, "no never will, no matter what nobody tells me, what your Uncle Hendreary saw fit to marry in a stuck-up thing like that Lupy."

"That's enough," said Pod. "We don't want none of that now."

He stood up and slung his borrowing-bag on his steel hat pin, swinging it over his shoulder. "Now," he asked, looking them up and down, "sure you're both all right?"

"Not that, when put to it," persisted Homily, "she isn't good-hearted at bottom, but it's the kind of way she does it . . ."

"What about your boots?" asked Pod. "They quite comfortable?"

"Yes," said Homily. "For the moment," she added.

"What about you, Arrietty?"

"I'm all right," said Arrietty.

"Because," said Pod, "it's going to be a long pull. We're going to take it steady. No need to rush. But we don't want no stopping. Nor no grumbling. Understand?"

"Yes," said Arrietty.

"And keep your eyes skinned," Pod went on as they all moved off along the path. "If you see anything, do as I do—and sharp, mind. We don't want no running every which way. We don't want no screaming."

"I know," said Arrietty irritably, adjusting her pack: she moved ahead as though trying to get out of earshot.

"You *think* you know," called Pod after her. "But you don't know nothing really: you don't know nothing about cover, nor does your mother: cover's a trained job, and art—like—"

"I know," repeated Arrietty. "You told me." She

glanced sideways into the shadowy depths of the brambles beside the path. She saw a great spider, hanging in space. His web was invisible: he seemed to be staring at her—she saw his eyes. Defiantly, Arrietty stared back.

"You can't tell no one in five minutes," persisted Pod, "things you got to learn from experience. What I told you, my girl, that day I took you out borrowing, wasn't even the A.B.C. I tried my best, because your mother asked me. And see where it's got us!"

"Now, Pod," panted Homily (they were walking too fast for her), "no need to bring up the past."

"That's what I mean," said Pod, "the past *is* experience: that's all you got to learn from. You see, when it comes to borrowing—"

"But you had a lifetime of it, Pod: you was in training—Arrietty'd only been out that once—"

"That's what I *mean*," cried Pod and, in stubborn desperation, he stopped in his tracks for Homily to catch up, "about cover. If only she'd known the A.B.C.—"

"Look out!" sang Arrietty shrilly, now some way ahead.

There was a rushing clatter, a dropped shadow and a hoarse, harsh cry: and, suddenly, there was Pod—alone on the path—face to face with a large black crow.

The bird stared wickedly, but a little distrustfully, his cramped toes turned in slightly, his great beak just open. Frozen to stillness Pod stared back: something growing in the path—that's what he looked like, a rather peculiar kind of chunky toadstool. The great bird, very curious, turned his head sideways and tried Pod with his other eye. Pod, motionless, stared back. The crow made a murmur in its throat—a tiny bleat and, puzzled, it moved forward. Pod let it come, a couple of sideways steps, and then—out of a still face—he spoke: "Get back to where you was," he said evenly, almost conversationally, and the bird seemed to hesitate. "We don't want no nonsense from you," Pod went on steadily. "Pigeon-toed, that's what you are! Crows is pigeon-toed; first time it struck me. Staring away like that, with one eye, and your head turned sideways . . . think it pretty, no doubt . . ." Pod spoke quite pleasantly ". . . but it ain't, not with *that* kind of beak . . ."

The bird became still, its expression no longer curious: there was stark amazement in every line of its rigid body and, in its eye, a kind of ghastly disbelief. "Go on! Get off with you!" shouted Pod suddenly, moving toward it. "Shoo . . . !" And, with a distraught glance and panic-stricken croak, the great bird flapped away. Pod wiped his brow with his sleeve as Homily, white-faced and still trembling, crawled out from under a foxglove leaf. "Oh, Pod," she gasped, "you were brave—you were wonderful!"

"It's nothing," said Pod. "It's a question of keeping your nerve."

"But the size of it!" said Homily. "You'd never think seeing them flying they was that size!"

"Size is nothing," said Pod. "It's the talk that gets them." He watched Arrietty climb out from a hollow stump and begin to brush herself down. When she looked up, he looked away. "Well," he said, after a moment, "we'd better keep moving . . ."

Arrietty smiled. She hesitated a moment, then ran across to him.

"What's that for?" asked Pod weakly as she flung

her arms round his neck. "Oh," cried Arrietty, hugging him. "You deserve a medal—the way you faced up to it, I mean."

"No, lass," said Pod, "you don't mean that: the way I was caught out, that's what you mean—caught out, good and proper, talking of cover." He patted her hand. "And, what's more, you're right: we'll face up to that one, too. You and your mother was trigger-quick and I'm proud of you." He let go her hand and swung his pack up onto his shoulders. "But another time, remember," he added, turning suddenly, "—not stumps. Hollow they may be but not always empty, see what I mean, and you're out of the frying pan into the fire. . . ."

On and on they went, following the path which the workmen had made when they dug out the trench for the gas pipe: it led them through two fields of pastureland, on a gradually rising slope alongside the hedge; they could walk with perfect ease under the lowest rung of any five-barred gate, picking a careful way across the clusters of sun-dried cattle tracks; these were craterlike but crumbling and Homily, staggering a little beneath her load, slipped once and grazed her knee.

On the third field, the gas pipe branched away obliquely to the left and Pod, looking ahead to where against the skyline he could just make out a stile, decided that they could safely now forsake the gas pipe and stick to the path beside the hedge. "Won't be so long now," he explained comfortingly when Homily begged to rest, "but we got to keep going. See that stile? That's what we're aiming for and we got to make it afore sunset."

So on they plodded and, to Homily, this last lap seemed the worst: her tired legs moved mechanically like scissors; stooping under her load, she was amazed each time she saw a foot come forward—it no longer seemed to be her foot; she would wonder vaguely how it got there.

Arrietty wished they could not see the stile: their tiny steps seemed to bring it no nearer; it worked better she found to keep her eyes on the ground and then every now and again if she looked up she could see they had made progress.

But at last they reached the crest of the hill: toward the right, on the far side of the cornfield beyond the hazel hedge, lay the woods, and ahead of them, after a slight dip, rose a vast sloping field, crossed with shadow from where the sun was setting behind the trees.

On the edge of this field, they stood and stared, awed by its vastness, its tilted angle against the rosy sky: on this endless sea of lengthening shadows and dreaming grassland, floated an island of trees dimmed already by its long thrown trail of dusk.

"This is it," said Pod, after a long moment. "Perkin's Beck." They stood, all three of them, underneath the stile, loath to lose its shelter.

"Perkin's what?" asked Homily uneasily.

"Perkin's Beck. You know—the name of the field. This is where they live, the Hendrearies."

"You mean," said Homily, after a pause, "where the badger's set is?"

"That's right," said Pod, staring ahead.

Homily's tired face looked yellow in the golden light; her jaw hung loose. "But where?" she asked.

Pod waved his arm. "Somewhere: it's in this field anyway."

"In this field . . ." repeated Homily dully, her eyes fixed on the dim boundaries, the distant group of shadowy trees.

"Well, we got to look," explained Pod uneasily. "You didn't think we'd go straight to it, did you?"

"I thought you knew where it was," said Homily. Her voice sounded husky. Arrietty, between them, stood strangely silent.

"Well, I brought you this far. Haven't I?" said Pod. "If the worse comes to the worst, we can camp for the night and look round in the morning."

"Where's the stream?" asked Arrietty. "There's supposed to be a stream."

"Well, there is," said Pod. "It flows down there, along that far hedge and then comes in like—do you see?—across that far corner. That thicker green there—can't you see? Them's rushes."

Arrietty screwed up her eyes. "Yes," she said uncertainly and added, "I'm thirsty."

"And so am I," said Homily. She sat down suddenly as though deflated. "All the way up that hill, step after step, hour after hour, I bin saying to meself, 'Never mind the first thing we'll do as soon as we get to that badger's set is sit down and have a nice cup o' tea'—it kept me going."

"Well, we will have one," said Pod. "Arrietty's got the candle."

"And I'll tell you another thing," went on Homily, staring ahead. "I couldn't walk across that there field, not if you offered me a monkey in a cage. We'll have to go round by the edges."

"Well, that's just what we're going to do," said Pod. "You don't find no badgers' sets in the middle of a field. We'll work round, systematic-like, bit by bit, starting out in the morning. But we got to sleep rough tonight, that's one thing certain. No good poking about tonight: it'll be dark soon: the sun's near off that hill already."

"And there are clouds coming up," said Arrietty, gazing at the sunset, "and moving fast."

"Rain?" cried Homily, in a stricken voice.

"Well, we'll move fast," said Pod, slinging his pack up. "Here, give me yours, Homily, you'll travel lighter . . ."

"Which way are we going?" asked Arrietty.

"We'll keep along by this lower hedge," said Pod, setting off. "And make toward the water. If we can't make it before the rain comes, we'll just take any shelter."

"What sort of shelter?" asked Homily, stumbling after him through the tussocky grass. "Look out, Pod, them's nettles!"

"I can see them," said Pod (they were walking in a shallow ditch). "A hole or something," he went on. "There's a hole there, for instance. See? Under that root."

Homily peered at it as she came abreast. "Oh, I couldn't go in there," she said. "There might be something in it."

"Or we could go right into the hedge," Pod called back.

"There's not much shelter in the hedge," said Arrietty. She walked alone, on the higher ground where the grass was shorter. "I can see from here: it's all stems and branches." She shivered a little in a sudden light wind which set the leaves of the hedge plants suddenly atremble, clashing the drying teasels as they swung and locked together. "It's clouding right over," she called.

"Yes, it'll be dark soon," said Pod. "You'd better come down here with us: you don't want to get lost."

"I won't get lost. I can see better from here. Look!" she called out suddenly. "There's an old boot. Wouldn't that do?"

"An old what?" asked Homily incredulously.

"Might do," said Pod, looking about him. "Where is it?"

"To your left. There. In the long grass . . ."

"An old boot!" cried Homily, as she saw him set down the borrowing-bags. "What's the matter with you, Pod—have you gone out of your mind?" Even as she spoke, it began to rain—great summer drops which bounced among the grasses.

"Take the borrowing-bags and get under that dock-leaf—both of you—while I look."

"An old boot—" repeated Homily incredulously, as she and Arrietty crouched under the dock-leaf: she had to raise her voice—the rain, on the swaying leaf, seemed to clatter rather than patter. "Hark at it!" complained Homily. "Come in closer, Arrietty, you'll catch your death. Oh, my goodness me—it's running down my back!"

"Look—he's calling to us," said Arrietty. "Come on!"

Homily bent her neck and peered out from under the swaying leaf. There stood Pod, some yards away, barely visible among the steaming grasses, dimmed by the curtain of rain. "A tropical scene," Arrietty thought, remembering her *Gazetteer of the World.* She thought of man against the elements, jungle swamps, steaming forests and Mr. Livingstone she presumed . . . "What's he want?" she heard her mother complaining. "We can't go out in this—look at it!"

"It's coming in underfoot now," Arrietty told her, "can't you see? This is a ditch. Come on, we must run for it; he's calling . . ."

They ran, half-crouching, stunned by the pounding water. Pod pulled them up into the longer grass, snatching Arrietty's borrowing-bag, gasping instructions, as they slid and slithered after him through what Arrietty thought of as "the bush."

"Here it is," said Pod. "Get in here."

The boot lay on its side: they had to crouch to enter. "Oh, my goodness," Homily kept saying. "Oh, my goodness me . . ." and would glance fearfully about the darkness inside. "I wonder who ever wore it."

"Go on," said Pod, "get further down. It's all right."

"No, no," said Homily. "I'm not going in no further: there might be something in the toe."

"It's all right," said Pod. "I've looked: there's nothing but a hole in the toe." He stacked the borrowing-bags against the inner side. "Something to lean against," he said.

"I wish I knew who'd wore this boot," Homily went on, peering about uncomfortably, wiping her wet face on her wetter apron.

"What good would that do you?" Pod said, untying the strings of the largest bag.

"Whether he was clean or dirty or what," said Homily, "and what he died of. Suppose he died of something infectious?"

"Why suppose he died?" said Pod. "Why shouldn't he be hale and hearty, and just had a nice wash and be sitting down to a good tea this very minute."

"Tea?" said Homily, her face brightening. "Where's the candle, Pod?"

"It's here," said Pod. "Give me a match, Arrietty, and a medium-sized aspirin lid. We got to go careful with the tea, you know: we got to go careful with everything."

Homily put out a finger and touched the worn leather. "I'll give this boot a good clean-out in the morning," she said.

"It's not bad," said Pod, taking out the half nail scissor. "If you ask me, we been lucky to find a boot like this. There ain't nothing to worry about: it's disinfected, all right—what with the sun and the wind and the rain year after year of it." He stuck the blade of the nail scissor through an eyelet hole and lashed it firm with a bit of old bootlace.

"What are you doing that for, Papa?" asked Arrietty.

"To stand the lid on, of course," said Pod. "A kind of bracket over the candle: we haven't got no tripod. Now you go and fill it with water, there's a good girl—there's plenty outside . . ."

There was plenty outside: it was coming down

in torrents; but the mouth of the boot faced out of the wind and there was a little dry patch before it. Arrietty filled the tin lid quite easily by tipping a large pointed foxglove leaf toward it so the rain ran off and down the point. All about her was the steady sound of rain and the lighted candle within the boot made the dusk seem darker. There was a smell of wildness, of space, of leaves and grasses and, as she turned away with the filled tin lid, another smell—winy, fragrant, spicy. Arrietty took note of it to remember it for morning—it was the smell of wild strawberries.

After they had drunk their hot tea and eaten a good half of sweet, crumbly digestive biscuit, they took off their wet outer clothes and hung them out along the handle of the nail scissor above the candle. Huddled together, with the old woolen sock about their shoulders, they talked a little. "Funny," Arrietty remarked, "to be wrapped in a sock and inside a boot." But Pod, watching the candle flame, was worried about wastage and, when the clothes had steamed a little, he doused the flame. Tired out, they lay down at last among the borrowing-bags, cuddled together for warmth. The last sound Arrietty heard as she fell asleep was the steady drumming of the rain on the hollow leather of the boot.

6

"Such is the tree, such is the fruit."
End of great railways strike at Peoria, Ill., 1891

[Extract from Arrietty's Diary and
Proverb Book, August 26th]

Arrietty was the first to wake. "Where am I?" she
wondered. She felt warm—too warm, lying there
between her mother and father—and when she turned
her head slightly she saw three little golden suns,
floating in the darkness. It was a second or two
before she realized what they were, and with this
knowledge memory flooded back—all that happened yesterday: the escape, the frenzied scramble
across the orchard, the weary climb, the rain. The
little golden suns, she realized, were the lace-holes
of the boot!

Stealthily Arrietty sat up: a balmy freshness stole
in upon her and, framed in the neck of the boot,
she saw the bright day: grasses, softly stirring, ten-
derly sunlit. Some were broken, where yesterday they
had pushed through them dragging the borrowing-
bags. There was a yellow buttercup—sticky and

gleaming, it looked, like wet paint. On a tawny stalk of sorrel, she saw an aphis—of a green so delicate that, against the sunlight, it looked transparent. "Ants milk them," Arrietty remembered, "perhaps we could."

She slid out from between her sleeping parents and just as she was, with bare feet and in her vest and petticoat, she ventured out-of-doors.

It was a glorious day: sunlit and rain-washed— the earth breathing out its scents. "This," Arrietty thought, "is what I have longed for; what I have imagined: what I knew existed—what I knew we'd have!"

She pushed through the grasses and soft drops of water fell on her benignly, warmed by the sun. Downhill a little way she went, toward the hedge, out of the jungle of higher grass, into the shallow ditch where, last night, the rain and darkness had combined to scare her.

There was warm mud here, between the shorter grass blades, fast-drying now in the sun. A bank rose between her and the hedge—a glorious bank, it was, filled with roots, with grasses, with tiny ferns, with small sandy holes, with violet leaves and with pale scarlet pimpernel, and, here and there, a globe of deeper crimson—wild strawberries!

She climbed the bank—leisurely and happily,

feeling the warm sun through her vest, her bare feet picking their way more delicately than clumsy human feet. She gathered three strawberries, heavy with juice, and ate them luxuriously, lying full-length on a sandy terrace before a mouse hole. From this bank she could see across the field, but today it looked different—as large, as ever; as oddly tilted; but alight and alive with the early sunshine. Now, all the shadows ran a different way—dewy, they seemed, on the gleaming golden grass. She saw in the distance the lonely group of trees: they still seemed to float on a grassy ocean. She thought of her mother's fear of open spaces. "But I could cross this field," she thought. "I could go anywhere . . ." Was this, perhaps, what Eggletina had thought? Eggletina—Uncle Hendreary's child—who, they said, had been eaten by the cat. Did enterprise, Arrietty wondered, always meet with disaster? Was it really better, as her parents had always taught her, to live in secret darkness underneath the floor?

The ants were out, she saw, and busy about their business—flurried, eager, weaving their anxious routes among the grass stems. Every now and again, Arrietty noticed, an ant waving its antennae would run up a grass stem and look around. A great contentment filled Arrietty: yes—here they were, for better or worse—there could be no going back!

Refreshed by the strawberries, she went on up the bank and into the shade of the hedge. Here was sunflecked greenness and a hollowness above her. Up and up as far as she could see—there were layers and stories of green chambers, crossed and re-crossed with springing branches. Cathedral-like, the hedge seemed from the inside.

Arrietty put her foot on a lower branch and swung herself up into the green shadows: quite easy, it was, with branches to her hand on all sides—easier than climbing a ladder. A ladder as high as this would mean a feat of endurance, and a ladder at best was a dull thing, whereas here was variety, a changing of direction, exploration of heights unknown. Some twigs were dry and rigid, shedding curls of dusty bark; others were lissom and alive with sap: on these, she would swing a little (as so often she had dreamed of swinging in that other lifetime under the floor!). "I will come here when it is windy," she told herself, "when the whole hedge is alive and swaying in the wind . . ."

Up and up, she went. She found an old bird's nest; the moss inside was straw-dry. She climbed into it and lay for a while and, leaning over the edge, dropped crumbled pieces of dried moss through the tangled branches below her; to watch them plummet between the boughs gave her, she found, an increased sense of height, a delicious giddiness which, safely in the nest, she enjoyed. But having felt this safety, climbing out and on and up seemed far more dangerous. "Suppose I fell," thought Arrietty, "as those bits of moss fell, skimming down through the shadowy hollows and banging and bouncing as they go?" But, as her hands closed round the friendly twigs and her toes spread a little to grip the bark, she was suddenly aware of her absolute safety—the ability (which for so long had been hidden deeply inside her) to climb. "It's heredity," she told herself. "That's why borrowers' hands and feet are longer in proportion than the hands and feet of human beings: that's how my father can come down by a fold in the tablecloth: how he can climb a curtain by the bobbles; how he can swing on his name-tape from a desk to a chair, from a chair to the floor. Just because I was a girl, and not allowed to go borrowing, it doesn't say I haven't got the gift . . ."

Suddenly, raising her head, she saw the blue sky above her, through the tracery of leaves—leaves which trembled and whispered as, in her haste, she swayed their stems. Placing her foot in a fork and swinging up, she caught her petticoat on a wild rose thorn and heard it rip. She picked the thorn out of the stuff and held it in her hand (it was the size to her of a rhinoceros horn to a human being): it was

light in proportion to its bulk, but very sharp and vicious-looking. "We could use this for something," Arrietty thought. "I must think . . . some kind of weapon . . ." One more pull and her head and shoulders were outside the hedge; the sun fell hot on her hair, and dazzled by the brightness, she screwed her eyes up as she gazed about her.

Hills and dales, valleys, fields and woods—dreaming in the sunshine. She saw there were cows in the next field but one. Approaching the wood, from a field on the lower side, she saw a man with a gun—very far away, he looked, very harmless. She saw the roof of Aunt Sophy's house and the kitchen chimney smoking. On the turn of a distant road, as it wound between the hedges, she saw a milk-cart: the sunlight flashed on the metal churn and she heard the faint fairylike tinkle of the harness brasses. What a world—mile upon mile, thing after thing, layer upon layer of unimagined richness—and she might never have seen it! She might have lived and died, as so many of her relations had done, in dusty twilight—hidden behind a wainscot.

Coming down, she found a rhythm: a daring swing, a letting go and a light drop into thickly clustered leaves which her instinct told her would act as a safety net, a cage of lissom twigs which sprang to hand and foot—lightly to be caught, lightly to be let go. Such leaves clustered more thickly toward the outside of the hedge, not in the bare hollows within, and her passage amongst them was almost like surf-riding—a controlled and bouncing slither. The last bough dropped her lightly on the slope of a grassy bank, springing back into place above her head, as lightly she let it go, with a graceful elastic shiver.

Arrietty examined her hands: one was slightly grazed. "But they'll harden up," she told herself. Her hair stood on end and was filled with bark dust, and there in her white embroidered petticoat she saw a great tear.

Hurriedly, she picked three more strawberries as a peace offering and, wrapping them in a violet leaf so as not to stain her vest, she scrambled down the bank, across the ditch, and into the clump of long grass.

Homily, at the entrance to the boot, looked worried as usual.

"Oh, Arrietty, where ever have you been? Breakfast's been ready this last twenty minutes. Your father's out of his mind!"

"Why?" asked Arrietty, surprised.

"With worrying about you—with looking for you."

"I was quite near," Arrietty said. "I was only in the hedge. You could have called me."

Homily put her finger on her lips and glanced in a fearful way from one side to another: "You can't *call*," she said, dropping her voice to an angry whisper. "We're not to make any noise at all, your father says. No calling or shouting—nothing to draw attention. Danger, that's what he said there is—danger on all sides . . ."

"I don't mean you have to whisper," Pod said, appearing suddenly from behind the boot, carrying the half nail scissor (he had been cutting a small trail through the thickest grass). "But don't you go off, Arrietty, never again without you say just where you're going and what for and for how long. Understand?"

"No," said Arrietty uncertainly. "I don't quite—I mean I don't always know what I'm going *for*—" (for what, for instance, had she climbed to the top of the hedge?) "Where is all this danger? I didn't see any. Excepting three cows two fields away."

Pod looked thoughtfully to where a sparrow hawk hung motionless in the clear sky.

"It's everywhere," he said, after a moment. "Before and Behind, Above and Below."

7

"Puff not against the Wind."
Oxford and Harvard Boat Race, 1869

[Extract from Arrietty's Diary and
Proverb Book, August 27th]

While Homily and Arrietty were finishing breakfast,
Pod got busy. He walked thoughtfully around the
boot, surveying it from different angles. He would
touch the leather with a practiced hand, peer at it
closely and then stand back, half-closing his eyes.
He removed the borrowing-bags, one by one, carefully stacking them on the grass outside and then
he crawled inside. They could hear him grunting
and panting a little as he knelt and stooped and
measured—he was, they gathered, making a carefully calculated examination of seams, joins, floor
space and quality of stitching.

After a while, he joined them as they sat there
on the grass. "Going to be a hot day," he said
thoughtfully, as he sat down, "a real scorcher." He
removed his necktie and heaved a sigh.

"What was you looking at, Pod?" asked Homily,
after a moment.

"You saw," said Pod. "That boot." He was silent a moment and then: "That's no tramp's boot," he said, "nor that boot weren't made for no working-man neither: that boot," went on Pod, staring at Homily, "is a gentleman's boot."

"Oh," breathed Homily in a relieved voice, half-closing her eyes and fanning her face with a limp hand. "Thank goodness for that!"

"Why, Mother?" asked Arrietty, irritated. "What's wrong with a workingman's boot? Papa's a working-man, isn't he?"

Homily smiled and shook her head in a pitying way. "It's a question," she said, "of quality."

"Your mother's right, there," said Pod. "Hand-sewn, that boot is, and as fine a bit of leather as ever I've laid me hand on." He leaned toward Arrietty. "And you see, lass, a gentleman's boot is well cared for, well greased and dubbined—years and years of it. If it hadn't been, don't you see, it would never have stood up—as this boot has stood up—to wind and rain and sun and frost. They pays dear for their boots, gentlemen do, but they sees they gets good value."

"That's right," agreed Homily, nodding her head and looking at Arrietty.

"Now, that hole in the toe," Pod went on. "I can patch that up with a bit of leather from the tongue. I can patch that up good and proper."

"It's not worth the time nor the thread," exclaimed Homily. "I mean to say, just for a couple o' nights or a day or two. It's not as though we were going to *live* in a boot," she pointed out, with an amused laugh.

Pod was silent a moment and then he said slowly, "I bin thinking."

"I mean to say," Homily went on, "we do know we got relations in this field and—though I wouldn't call a badger's set much of a home, mind—at least it's somewhere."

Pod raised solemn eyes. "Maybe," he said, in the same grave voice. "But all the same, I bin thinking. I've bin thinking," he went on, "relations or no relations, they're still borrowers, ain't they? And among human beings, for instance, who ever sees a borrower?" He gazed round challengingly.

"Well, that boy did—" began Arrietty, "and—"

"Ah," said Pod, "because you, Arrietty, who wasn't no borrower—who hadn't even learned to borrow—went up and talked to him: sought him out, shameless—knowing no better. And I told you just what would happen, hunted out, I said we'd be, by cats and ratcatchers—by policemen and all. Now was I right or wasn't I?"

"Yes, you were right," said Arrietty, "but—"

"There ain't no buts," said Pod. "I was right. And if I was right then, I'm right now. See? I bin thinking and what I've bin thinking is right—and, this time, there ain't going to be no nonsense from you. Nor from your mother, neither."

"There won't be no nonsense from me, Pod," said Homily in a pious voice.

"Now," said Pod, "this is how it strikes me. Human beings stand high and move fast; when you stand higher you can see farther—do you get me? What I mean to say is—if, with them advantages, a human being can't never find a borrower . . . even goes as far as to say they don't believe borrowers *exist*—why should we borrowers, who stand lower and move slower compared to them like, hope to do much better? Living in a house, say, with several families—well, of course, we know each other . . . stands to reason: we been brought up together. But come afield, to a strange place like this and—this is how it seems to me—borrowers is hid from borrowers."

"Oh, my," said Homily unhappily.

"We don't move 'slow' exactly," said Arrietty.

"Compared to them, I said. Our legs move *fast* enough—but theirs is longer. Look at the ground they cover!" He turned to Homily. "Now don't upset yourself. I don't say we won't find the Hendrearies—

Maybe, we will . . . quite soon. Or anyway before
the winter—"

"The winter . . ." breathed Homily in a stricken
voice.

"But we got to plan," went on Pod, "and act,
as though there weren't no badger's set. Do you see
what I mean?"

"Yes, Pod," said Homily huskily.

"I bin thinking it out," he repeated. "Here we
are, the three of us, with what we got in the bags,
two hat pins and an old boot: we got to face up to
it and, what's more—" he added solemnly, "we got
to live different."

"How different?" asked Homily.

"Cold food, for instance. No more hot tea. No coffee. We got to keep the candle and the matches in hand for winter. We got to look about us and see what there is."

"Not caterpillars, Pod," pleaded Homily. "You promised! I couldn't never eat a caterpillar . . ."

"Nor you shall," said Pod, "not if I can help it. There's other things this time o' year, plenty. Now, I want you to get up, the two of you, and see how this boot drags—"

"How do you mean?" asked Homily, mystified, but obediently they both stood up.

"See these laces?" said Pod. "Good and strong—been oiled, that's why . . . or tarred. Now, you each take a lace over your shoulder and pull. Turn your back to the boot . . . that's right . . . and just walk forward."

Homily and Arrietty leaned on the traces and the boot came on with a bump and a slither so fast across the slippery grass that they stumbled and fell—they had not expected it would be so light.

"Steady on!" cried Pod, running up beside them. "Take it steady, can't you . . . Up you get . . . That's the way . . . Steady, steady . . . That's fine. You see," he said when they paused for breath, having dragged the boot to the edge of the long grass, "how it goes—like a bird!" Homily and Arrietty rubbed their shoulders and said nothing: they even smiled slightly, a pale reflection of Pod's pride and delight. "Now, sit down, both of you. You was fine. Now, you'll see, this is going to be good—"

He stood, beaming down at them as, meekly, they sat on the grass. "It's like this—" he explained. "I talked just now of danger—to you, Arrietty, and that's because, though brave we must be (and there's none braver than your mother when she's put to it) we can't never be foolhardy. We got to make our plans and we got to keep our heads. We can't afford to waste no energy—climbing hedges just for fun, and suchlike—and we can't afford to take no risks.

We got to make our plan and we got to stick to it. Understand?"

"Yes," said Arrietty, and Homily nodded her head. "Your father's right," she said.

"You got to have a main object," went on Pod, "and ours is there, ready-made—we got to find the badger's set. Now how are we going to set about it? It's a big field—take us the best part of a day to get along one side of it, let alone have time to look down holes; and we'd be wore out, that's what we'd be. Say I went off looking by myself—well, your mother would never know a moment's peace all day long, till she had me safe back again. There's nothing bad enough for what she'd be imagining. *And* going on at you, Arrietty. Now, that's all wear and tear, and we can't afford too much of it. Folk get silly when they're fussed, if you see what I mean, and that's when accidents happen.

"Now, my idea," Pod went on, "is this. We'll work our way all round this field, like I said last night, by the edges—"

"Hedges," corrected Arrietty, under her breath, without thinking.

"I heard what you said, Arrietty," remarked Pod quietly (he seldom grudged her superior education). "There's hedges and edges, and I meant edges . . ."

"Sorry," murmured Arrietty, blushing.

"As I was saying," Pod went on, "we'll work our way round, systematic-like, exploring the banks and—" he looked at Arrietty pointedly, "hedges—and camping as we go: a day here, a day or two there, just as we feel; or depending on the holes and burrows. There'll be great bits of bank where there couldn't be no badger's set—we can skip those, as you might say. Now you see, Homily, we couldn't do this if we had a settled home."

"You mean," asked Homily sharply, "that we've got to drag the boot?"

"Well," said Pod, "was it heavy?"

"With all our gear in it, it would be."

"Not over grass," said Pod.

"And uphill!" exclaimed Homily.

"*Level* here at the bottom of the field," corrected Pod patiently, "as far as them rushes; then uphill at the top of the field, alongside the stream: then across—*level* again; then the last lap of all, which brings us back to the stile again, and it's downhill all the way!"

"Um-m-m," said Homily, unconvinced.

"Well," said Pod. "Out with it—speak your mind: I'm open to suggestions."

"Oh, Mother—" began Arrietty in a pleading voice and then became silent.

"Has Arrietty and me got to drag all the time?" asked Homily.

"Now, don't be foolish," said Pod. "We take it in turns, of course."

"Oh, well," sighed Homily, "what can't be cured, needs must."

"That's my brave old girl," said Pod. "Now about provender—(*food*," he explained as Homily looked up bewildered). "We better become vegetarians, pure and simple, one and all, and make no bones about it."

"There won't be no bones to make," remarked Homily grimly, "not if we become vegetarians."

"The nuts is coming on," said Pod. "Nearly ripe they'll be down in that sheltered corner—milky like. Plenty of fruit—blackberries, them wild strawberries. Plenty of salad, dandelion, say, and sorrel. There's gleanings still in that cornfield t'other side of the stile. We'll manage—the thing is you got to get used to it: no hankering for boiled ham, chicken rissoles, and that kind of fodder. Now, Arrietty," he went on, "as you're so set on hedge climbing, you and your mother had better go off and gather us some nuts. How's that, eh? And I'll get down to a bit of cobbling." He glanced at the boot.

"Where do you find the nuts?" asked Arrietty.

"There, about halfway along"—Pod pointed to

a thickening of pale green in the hedge—"before you get to the water. You climb up, Arrietty, and throw 'em down and your mother can gather 'em up. I'll come down and join you later: we got to dig a pit."

"A pit? Whatever for?" asked Arrietty.

"We can't carry that weight of nuts around," explained Pod, "not in a boot this size. Wherever we find provender, we got to make a cache like, and mark it down for winter."

"Winter . . ." moaned Homily softly in the bleak voice she reserved for that season.

Nevertheless, as Arrietty helped her mother over the rough places in the ditch which because it was shallow, well drained and fairly sheltered could be used as a highway, she felt closer to Homily than she had felt for years—more like a sister, as she put it. "Oh, look," cried Homily when she saw a scarlet pimpernel. She stopped and picked it by its hair-thin stalk. "Isn't it lovely?" she said in a tender voice; touching the fragile petals with a work-worn finger, she tucked it into the opening of her blouse. Arrietty found a pale blue counterpart in the delicate bird's-eye, and put it in her hair; and suddenly the day began to seem like a holiday. "Flowers made for borrowers . . ." she thought.

At last they reached the nutty part of the hedge.

"Oh, Arrietty," exclaimed Homily, gazing up at the spreading branches with mingled pride and fear, "you can't never go up there."

But Arrietty could and would: she was delighted to show off her climbing: in a workmanlike manner, she stripped off her jersey, hung it on a gray-green spike of thistle, rubbed her palms together (in front of Homily she did not like to spit on them) and clambered up the bank.

Homily watched below, her two hands clasped and pressed against her heart, how the outer leaves shivered and shook as Arrietty, invisible, climbed up inside. "Are you all right?" she kept calling, "oh, Arrietty, do be careful. Suppose you fell and broke your leg?" And then after a while the nuts began to come down and poor Homily, under fire, ran this way and that, in her panting efforts to retrieve them.

Not that they came down fast enough to be really dangerous. Nut gathering was not quite as easy as Arrietty had imagined. For one thing, it was still a little early in the season and the nuts were not quite ripe. Each was still encased in what, to Arrietty, looked something like a tough, green foxglove bell and was fixed firmly to the tree. It was quite an effort, until she learned the trick of a sharp twist, for Arrietty to detach the clusters. And what was more, even to reach them was not easy. It meant climbing or swinging or edging her body along a perilously swaying branch tip (later Pod made her— out of a piece of lead, some twine and a supple dock root—a kind of swinging cosh with which she could strike them down) but she persevered and soon there was a sizable pile in the ditch, neatly stacked up by the perspiring Homily.

"That'll do now," Homily called out breathlessly after a while. "No more or your poor pa will never get through with the digging," and Arrietty, hot and disheveled, with scratched face and smarting hands, thankfully climbed down. She flung herself full length in the speckled shade of a clump of cow parsley and complained of feeling thirsty.

"Well, there's water farther along, so your pa says. Do you think you could walk it?"

Of course Arrietty could walk it: tired, she might be but determined to foster this newfound spirit of adventure in her mother. She caught up her jersey and they set off along the ditch.

The sun was higher now and the ground was hotter. They came to a place where some beetles were eating a long-dead mole. "Don't look," said Homily, quickening her step and averting her eyes, as though it were a street accident.

But Arrietty, more practical for once, said, "But when they've finished, perhaps we ought to have the skin. It might come in useful," she pointed out, "for winter."

"Winter . . ." breathed Homily, "you say it to torment me," she added in a sudden spurt of temper. The stream when they reached it seemed less a stream than a small clear pond disturbed as they approached by several plops and spreading silvery circles as the frogs, alarmed, dived in. It meandered out of a tangled wood beyond the hedge and, crossing the corner of the field, had spread into a small marsh of cresses, mud and deep-sunk cattle tracks. On the farther side of the stream, the field was bounded, not by a junction of hedges but by several mildewed posts hung with rusty wire slung across the water. Beyond this frail barrier, the shadowed tree trunks of the wood seemed to crowd and glower as though they longed to rush forward across the strip of water into the field and the sunlight. Arrietty saw a powdery haze of wild forget-me-not, with here and there a solitary bulrush. The dry-edged cattle tracks were water-filled chasms crisscrossed with dikes, and there was a delicious smell of fragrant slime, lightly spiced with spearmint. A sinuous, feathered current of clear ripples broke the still, sky-reflecting surface of the miniature lake. It was very beautiful, Arrietty thought, and strangely exciting; she had never seen so much water before.

"Watercress!" announced Homily in a flat voice. "We'll take a bit o' that for tea . . ."

They picked their way along the raised ridges of the cow craters whose dark pits of stagnant water reflected the cloudless sky. Arrietty stooping over them saw her own clear image sharply focused against the dreaming blue but oddly tilted and somehow upside down.

"Careful you don't fall in, Arrietty," warned Homily. "You only got one change, remember. You know," she went on in an interested voice, pointing at a bulrush, "I could have used one of those back home, under the kitchen. Just the thing for cleaning out the flues. Wonder your father never thought of it. And don't drink yet," advised Homily (as though Arrietty intended to!). "Wait till we get where the water's running. Same with watercress, you don't want to pick it where the water's stagnant. You never know what you might get."

At last they found a place from where it would be possible to drink: a solid piece of bark, embedded firmly in the mud yet stretching out into the stream forming a kind of landing stage or rough jetty. It was gray and nobbly and looked like a basking crocodile. Arrietty stretched her length on the corklike surface and cupping her hands took long draughts of the cool water. Homily, after some hesitation and arrangements of skirts, did the same. "Pity," she remarked, "we don't have a jug nor a pail, nor some kind of bottle. We could do with some water in the boot."

Arrietty did not reply; she was gazing happily down past the drifting surface into the depths below.

"Can vegetarians eat fish?" she asked, after a while.

"I don't rightly know," said Homily. "We'll have to ask your father." Then the cook in Homily reasserted itself. "Are there any?" she asked, a trifle hungrily.

"Plenty," Arrietty murmured dreamily, gazing down into the shifting depths. The stream, she thought, seemed to be gently breathing. "About as long as my forearm. And some invisible things," she added, "like shrimps. . . ."

"How do you mean—*invisible*?" asked Homily.

"Well," explained Arrietty in the same absent voice, "I mean you can see through them. And some black things," she went on, "like blobs of expanding velvet. . . ."

"Leeches, I shouldn't wonder," remarked Homily with a slight shudder, and added dubiously, after a moment's thought, "Might be all right stewed."

"Do you think Papa could make a fishing net?" asked Arrietty.

"Your father can make anything," asserted Homily loyally. "No matter what—you've only got to name it."

Arrietty lay quiet for a while, dozing, she seemed, on this sun-soaked piece of bark, and when at last she spoke Homily gave a startled jump—she, too, lulled for once into quietness, had begun to float away. Never do, she thought, to drop off to sleep on a log like this. You might turn over. And she roused herself by an inward shake and rapidly blinked her eyes.

"What did you say, Arrietty?" she asked.

"I said . . ." Arrietty went on after a moment in a lilting lazy voice, "couldn't we bring the boot down here? Right beside the water?"

8

"Every man's house is his castle."
Oxford and Harvard Boat Race, 1869

[Extract from Arrietty's Diary and
Proverb Book, August 27th]

And that is just what they did do. Pod, consulted,
had looked over the site, weighed the pros and cons
and rather ponderously as though it was his own
idea decided they should move camp. They would
choose a site further along the hedge as near as was
safe to the brook. "Homily can do her washing. You
got to have water," he announced, but rather de-
fensively as though he had only just thought of it.
"And I might make a fish net, at that."

The boot, though fully loaded, ran quite easily
along the shallow ditch with all three of them in
harness. The site Pod had chosen was a platform or
alcove halfway up the steepish bank below the hedge.

"You want to keep fairly high," he explained
(as, to make it lighter for hauling, they unpacked
the boot in the ditch), "with rain like we had the
other night and the brook so near. You got to remember," he went on, selecting a sharp tool, "that

flood we had back home when the kitchen boiler burst."

"What do you mean," sniffed Homily, " 'got to remember'? Scalding hot, that one was, too." She straightened her back and gazed up the slope at the site.

It was well chosen: a kind of castle, Arrietty had called it, in which they would live in the dungeons, but in their case the dungeon was more like an alcove, open to the sun and air. A large oak tree, at one time part of the hedge, had been sawn off at the base. Solid and circular, it stood up above the bank where the hedge thinned, like the keep of a fortress, its roots flung out below as flying buttresses. Some of these were not quite dead and had shot forth here and there a series of suckers like miniature oak trees. One of these saplings overhung their cave, shading its lip with sun-flecked flickering shadow.

The underside of a large root formed the roof of their alcove and other smaller roots supported the walls and floor. These, Pod pointed out, would come in handy as beams and shelves.

He was busy now (while the boot still lay in the ditch) extracting some nails from the heel.

"It seems a shame," remarked Homily as she

and Arrietty sorted out belongings for easier transportation. "You'll lose the whole heel."

"What good's the heel to us?" asked Pod, perspiring with effort. "We ain't going to wear the boot. And I need the nails," he added firmly.

The flat top of the tree trunk, they decided, would come in useful as a lookout, a bleaching ground for washing, and a place for drying herbs and fruit. Or for grinding corn. Pod was urged to chip out footholds in the trunk for easier climbing. (This he did later and for years after these footholds were considered by naturalists to be the work of the great spotted woodpecker.)

"We got to dig a cache for these nuts," remarked Pod, straightening his aching back, "but better we get all shipshape here first and snug for the night, as you might say. Then after the digging we can come home straight to bed."

Seven nails, Pod decided, was enough for the moment (it was tough work extracting them). The idea had come to him when he had been mending the hole in the toe. Heretofore, he had only worked on the softest of glove leathers and his little cobbler's needle was too frail to pierce the tough hide of the boot. Using the electric bell-clapper as a hammer, he had pierced (with the help of a nail) a series of

matching holes in the boot itself and the tongue which was meant to patch it: then all he had to do was to thread in some twine.

By the same token, he had made a few eyelet holes round the ankle of the boot so they could, if necessary, lash it up at night—as campers would close a tent flap.

It did not take them long to drag the empty boot up the slope, but wedging it firmly in the right position under the main root of the alcove was a tricky business and took a good deal of maneuvering. At last it was done—and they left panting but relieved.

The boot lay on its side, sole against the rear wall and ankle facing outwards so that if disturbed at night they could spot the intruder approaching, and so when they woke in the morning they would get the early sun.

Pod drove a series of nails along one shelflike root on the right wall of the alcove (the left wall was almost completely taken up by the boot) on which he hung his tools: the half nail scissor, the fretsaw, the bell-clapper, and the piece of razor blade.

Above this shelf was a sandy recess which Homily could use as a larder. It went in quite deep.

When Pod had placed the larger hat pin in a place of strategic importance near the mouth of the alcove (the smaller one they were to keep in the boot in case, Pod said, "of these alarms at night") they felt they had met the major demands of the moment and, though tired, they felt a pleasant sense of achievement and of effort well spent.

"Oh, my back," exclaimed Homily, her hands in the small of it. "Let's just sit down, Pod, for a moment and rest quietly and look at the view." And it was worth looking at in the afternoon sunlight. They could see right away across the field. A pheasant flew out of the far group of trees and whirred away to the left.

"We can't sit down now," said Pod. "We got to dig that cache."

Wearily, they collected the half nail scissor and a borrowing-bag for anything they might see on the way, and the three of them climbed down the bank.

"Never mind," Pod comforted Homily as they made their way along the ditch. "We can go straight to bed after. And you haven't got no cooking," he reminded her.

Homily was not comforted. As well as tired she realized suddenly she was feeling very hungry (but not,—she reflected glumly—somehow, for nuts).

When they reached the place and Pod had removed the first sods in order to reach the soil (great shrubs these were to him, like uprooting a clump of pampas), Homily revived a little—determined to play her part (courageous helpmate, it was today). She had never dug before, but the prospect faintly excited her. Strange things are possible in this odd world and she might (one never knew) discover a new talent.

They had to take it in turns with the half nail scissor. ("Never mind," Pod told them. "I'll set to work tomorrow and rig us up a couple of spades.")

Homily screamed when she saw her first worm: it was as long as she was—even longer, she realized, as the last bit wriggled free. "Pick it up," said Pod, "it won't hurt you. You got to learn." And, before Arrietty (who was not too keen on worms herself) could volunteer to help, she saw her mother, with set face and tensed muscles, lay hold of the writhing creature and drop it some inches beyond the hole where it writhed gratefully away among the grasses. "It was heavy," Homily remarked—her only comment—and she went back to her digging; but (Arrietty thought) she looked a trifle pale. After her third worm, Homily became slightly truculent—she handled it with the professional casualness of an experienced snake charmer—almost bored, she seemed. Arrietty was much impressed. It was a dif-ferent story, however, when her mother dug up a centipede—then Homily not only screamed but ran, clutching her skirts, halfway up the bank, where she stood on a flat stone, almost gibbering. She only consented to rejoin them when Pod, tickling the angry squirming insect with the tip of the nail scissor, sent it scuttling at last into what Arrietty always thought of as "the bush."

They carried a few nuts home for supper: these, and several wild strawberries, a leaf or two of watercress, washed down with cold water, made an adequate though somehow dismal repast. There seemed to be something lacking; a bit of digestive biscuit would have been nice, or a good cup of hot tea. But the last piece of biscuit, Homily decided, must be kept for breakfast and the tea (Pod had ordained) only for celebrations and emergencies.

But they slept well all the same; and felt safe, tucked away under their protecting root, with the boot laced up in front. It was a little airless, perhaps, but they were far less cramped for space because so many of their belongings could be stacked outside now in the sandy, root-filled annex.

9

"As ye sow, so shall ye reap."
Valparaiso surrenders to
the Congressionalists, 1891

[Extract from Arrietty's Diary and
Proverb Book, August 28th]

"Now, today," said Pod, at breakfast next morning, "we'd better go gleaning. There's a harvested cornfield yonder. Nuts and fruit is all right," he went on, "but for winter we're going to need bread."

"Winter?" moaned Homily. "Aren't we supposed to be looking for the badger's set? And," she went on, "who's going to grind the corn?"

"You and Arrietty, couldn't you?" said Pod. "Between two stones."

"You'll be asking us to make fire with two sticks next," grumbled Homily, "and how do you think I can make bread without an oven? And what about yeast? Now, if you ask me," she went on, "we don't want to go gleaning and trying to make bread and all that nonsense: what we want to do is to put a couple of nuts in our pockets, pick what fruit we see on the way, and have a real good look for the badger's set."

"As you say," agreed Pod, after a moment, and heaved a sigh.

They tidied away breakfast, put the more precious of their belongings inside the boot and carefully laced it up, and struck out uphill, beyond that water, along the hedge which lay at right angles to the bank in which they had passed the night.

It was a weary traipse. Their only adventure was at midday, when they rested after a frugal luncheon of rain-sodden, overripe blackberries. Homily, lying back against the bank, her drowsy eyes fixed on the space between a stone and a log, saw the ground begin to move: it streamed past the gap, in a limited but constant flow.

"Oh, my goodness, Pod," she breathed, after watching a moment to make sure it was not an optical illusion, "do you see what I see? There, by that log . . ." Pod, following the direction of her eyes, did not speak straight away and when he did, it was hardly above a whisper.

"Yes," he said, seeming to hesitate. "It's a snake."

"Oh, my goodness . . ." breathed Homily again in a trembling voice, and Arrietty's heart began to beat wildly.

"Don't move," whispered Pod, his eyes on the steady ripple: there seemed to be no end—the snake went on and on and on (unless it was, as Arrietty thought afterwards, that Time itself, in a moment of danger, has often been said to slow down) but just when they felt they could bear the sight not a moment longer, they saw the flick of its tail.

They all breathed again. "What was it, Pod?" asked Homily weakly, "an adder?"

"A grass snake, I think," said Pod.

"Oh," exclaimed Arrietty, with a relieved little laugh, "they're harmless."

Pod looked at her gravely; his currant-bunnish face seemed more doughy than usual. "To humans," he said slowly. "And what's more," he added, "you can't talk to snakes."

"Pity," remarked Homily, "that we did not bring one of the hat pins."

"What good would that have done?" asked Pod.

By about tea time (rose hips, this time: they were sick of sodden blackberries) they found, to their surprise, that they were more than halfway along the third side of the field. There had been more walking than searching: none of the ground they had covered so far could have housed the Hendrearies let alone a badger colony. The bank, as they made their way uphill beside the hedge, had become lower in proportion until, here where they sat drearily munching rose hips, there was no bank at all.

"It's almost as far now," said Pod, "to go back the same way as we came as to keep on round. What do you say, Homily?"

"We better keep on round, then," said Homily hoarsely, a hairy seed of a rose hip being stuck in her throat. She began to cough. "I thought you said you cleaned them?" she complained to Arrietty, when she could get back her breath.

"I must have missed one," said Arrietty. "Sorry," and she passed her mother a new half hip, freshly scoured; she had rather enjoyed opening the pale scarlet globes and scooping out the golden nest of close-packed seeds, and she liked the flavor of the hips themselves—they tasted, she thought, of apple skins honeyed over with a dash of rose petal.

"Well, then," said Pod, standing up, "we better start moving."

The sun was setting when they reached the fourth and last side of the field; but the hedge threw out a ragged carpet of shadow. Through a gap in the dark branches they could see a blaze of golden light on a sea of harvested stubble.

"As we're here," suggested Pod, standing still and staring through the gap, "and it's pretty well downhill most the way back now, what's the harm in an ear or two of corn?"

"None," said Homily wearily, "if it would walk out and follow us."

"Corn ain't heavy," said Pod. "Wouldn't take us no time to pick up a few ears. . ."

Homily sighed. It was she who had suggested this trip, after all. In for a penny, she decided wanly, in for a pound.

"Have it your own way," she said resignedly.

So they clambered through the hedge and into the cornfield.

And into a strange world (as it seemed to Arrietty) not like the Earth at all: the golden stubble, lit by the evening sun, stood up in rows like a blasted colorless forest; each separate bole threw its own long shadow and all the shadows, combed by the sun in direction, lay parallel—a bizarre crisscross of light and dark which flicked and fleckered with every footstep. Between the boles, on the dry straw-strewn earth, grew scarlet pimpernel in plenty, with here and there a ripened ear of wheat.

"Take a bit of stalk, too," Pod advised them. "Makes it easier to carry."

The light was so strange in this broken, beetle-haunted forest that, every now and again, Arrietty seemed to lose sight of her parents but, turning panic-stricken, would find them again quite close, zebra-striped with black and gold.

At last they could carry no more and Pod had mercy; they forgathered on their own side of the hedge, each with two hunches of wheat ears, carried head downwards by a short length of stalks. Arrietty was reminded of Crampfurl, back home in the big house, going past the grating with onions for the kitchen; they had been strung on strings and looked like these corn grains and in about the same proportion.

"Can you manage all that?" asked Pod anxiously of Homily as she started off ahead down the hill.

"I'd sooner carry it than grind it," remarked Homily tartly, without looking back.

"There wouldn't be no badgers' sets along this side," panted Pod (he was carrying the heaviest load), coming abreast of Arrietty. "Not with all the plowing, sowing, dogs, men, horses, tractors and whatnot—as there must have been—"

"Where could one be, then?" asked Arrietty, setting down her corn for a moment to rest her hands. "We've been all round."

"There's only one place to look, now," said Pod. "Them trees in the middle," and standing still in the deep shadow, he gazed across the stretch of pastureland. The field looked in this light much as it had on that first day (could that only be the day before yesterday?). But from this angle, they could not see the trail of dusky shadow thrown by the island of trees.

"Open ground," said Pod, staring. "Your mother would never make it."

"I'd go," said Arrietty. "I'd like to go. . . ."

Pod was silent. "I got to think," he said, after a moment. "Come on, lass. Take up your corn, else we won't get back before dark."

They didn't. Or, rather, it was deep dusk along the ditch of their home stretch and almost dark when they came abreast of their cave. But even in the half-light there seemed something suddenly home-like and welcoming about the laced-up boot.

Homily sank down at the foot of the bank, between her bunches of corn. "Just a breather—" she explained weakly, "before that next pull up."

"Take your time," said Pod. "I'll go ahead and unlace the boot." Panting a little, half-dragging his ears of corn, he started up the bank. Arrietty followed.

"Pod," called Homily from the darkness below, without turning, "you know what?"

"What?" asked Pod.

"It's been a long day," said Homily. "Suppose, tonight, we made a nice cup of tea."

"Please yourself," said Pod, unlacing the neck

of the boot and feeling cautiously inside. He raised his voice, shouting down at her: "What you have now, you can't have later. Bring the half scissor, Arrietty, will you? It's on a nail in the storeroom." After a moment, he added impatiently, "Hurry up. No need to take all day, it's just there to your hand."

"It isn't," came Arrietty's voice, after a moment.

"What do you mean—it isn't?"

"It isn't here. Everything else is, though."

"Isn't there!" exclaimed Pod unbelievingly. "Wait a minute, let *me* look." Their voices sounded muffled to Homily, listening below; she wondered what the fuss was about.

"Something or someone's been mucking about in here," she heard Pod say, after what seemed a distressed pause; and picking up her ears of wheat Homily scrambled up the bank.

"Get a match, will you," Pod was saying in a worried voice, "and light the candle," and Homily foraged in the boot to find the wax matches.

As the wick guttered, wavered, then rose to a steady flame, the little hollow, halfway up the bank, became illumined like a scene on a stage: strange shadows were cast on the sandy walls of the annex. Pod and Homily and little Arrietty seemed, as they passed back and forth, curiously unreal, like characters in a play. There were the borrowing-bags, stacked neatly together as Pod had left them, their mouths tied up with twine; there hung the tools from their beamlike root, and, leaning beside them—as Pod had left it this morning—the purple thistle-head with which he had swept the floor. He stood there now, white-faced in the candlelight, his hand on a bare nail. "It was here," he said, tapping the nail, "that's where I left it."

"Oh, goodness," exclaimed Homily, setting down her wheat ears. "Let's just look again." She pulled aside the borrowing-bags and felt behind them. "And you, Arrietty," she ordered, "could you get round to the back of the boot?"

But it was not there nor, they discovered suddenly, was the larger hat pin. "Anything but them two things," Pod kept saying in a worried voice as Homily, for the third or fourth time, went through the contents of the boot. "The smaller hat pin's here all right," she kept repeating. "We still got one. You see no animal could unlace a boot. . . ."

"But what kind of animal," asked Pod wearily, "would take a half nail scissor?"

"A magpie might," suggested Arrietty, "if it looked kind of shiny."

"Maybe," said Pod. "But what about the hat pin? I don't see a magpie carrying the two. No," he went on thoughtfully, "it doesn't look to me like no magpie, nor like any other race of bird. Nor no animal neither, if it comes to that. Nor I wouldn't say it was any kind of human being: a human being, like as not, finding a hole like this smashes the whole place up. Kind of kick with their feet, human beings do out walking, 'fore they touch a thing with their hands. Looks to me," said Pod, "like something in the style of a borrower."

"Oh," cried Arrietty joyfully, "then we've found them!"

"Found what?" asked Pod.

"The cousins . . . the Hendrearies . . ."

Pod was silent a moment. "Maybe," he said uneasily again.

"Maybe!" mimicked Homily, irritated. "Who else could it be? They live in this field, don't they? Arrietty, put some water on to boil, there's a good girl. We don't want to waste the candle."

"Now see here—" began Pod.

"But we can't fix the tin lid," interrupted Arrietty, "without something to hold it."

"Oh, goodness me," complained Homily, "use your head and think of something! Suppose we'd never had a nail scissor! Tie a piece of twine round an aspirin lid and hang it over the flame from a nail or bit of root or something. What were you saying, Pod?"

"I said we got to go careful on the tea, that's all. We was only going to make tea to celebrate like, or in what you might call a case of grave emergency."

"Well, we are, aren't we?"

"Are what?" asked Pod.

"Celebrating. Looks like we've found what we come for."

Pod glanced uneasily toward Arrietty who, in the farther corner of the annex, was busily knotting twine round a ridged edge of a screw-on lid. "You don't want to go so fast, Homily," he warned her, lowering his voice, "nor you don't want to jump to no conclusions. Say it was one of the Hendrearies. All right, then, why didn't they leave a word or sign or stay awhile and wait for us? Hendreary knows our gear all right—that Proverb book of Arrietty's, say, many's the time he's seen it back home under the kitchen."

"I don't see what you're getting at," said Homily in a puzzled voice, watching Arrietty anxiously as gingerly she suspended the water-filled aspirin lid from a root above the candle. "Careful," she called out. "You don't want to burn the twine."

"What I'm getting at is this," explained Pod. "Say you look at the nail scissor as a blade, a sword—as you might say—and the hat pin as a spear, say, or a dagger. Well, whoever took them things has armed himself, see what I mean? And left us weaponless."

"We got the other hat pin," said Homily in a troubled voice.

"Maybe," said Pod. "But he doesn't know that, see what I mean?"

"Yes," whispered Homily, very scared.

"Make tea, if you like," Pod went on, "but I wouldn't call it a celebration. Not yet, at any rate."

Homily glanced unhappily toward the candle: above the aspirin lid, she noticed longingly, already there rose a welcome haze of steam. "Well," she began and hesitated. Then suddenly she seemed to brighten. "It comes to the same thing."

"How do you mean?" asked Pod.

"About the tea," explained Homily, perking up. "Going by what you said, stealing our weapons and such—this looks to be something you might call serious. Depends how it strikes you. I mean," she went on hurriedly, "there's some I know as might even name it a state of grave emergency."

"There's some as might," agreed Pod wanly. Then, suddenly, he sprang aside, beating the air with his hands. Arrietty screamed and Homily, for a second, thought they had both gone mad. Then she saw.

A great moth had lumbered into the alcove, attracted by the candle; it was fawn-colored and, to Homily, hideous, drunk and blinded with light. "Save the tea—" she cried, panic-stricken, and seizing the purple thistle-head, beat wildly about the air. Shadows danced every way and, in their shouting and scolding, they hardly noticed a sudden, silent thickening of night swerve in on the dusk; but they felt the wind of its passing, watched the candle gutter, and saw the moth was gone.

"What was that?" asked Arrietty at last, after an awed silence.

"It was an owl," said Pod. He looked thoughtful.

"It ate the moth?"

"As it would eat you," said Pod, "if you went mucking about after dusk. We're living and learning," he said. "No more candles after dark. Up with the sun and down with the sun: that's us, from now on."

"The water's boiling, Pod," said Homily.

"Put the tea in," said Pod, "and douse the light: we can drink all right in the dark," and turning away he propped the broom handle back against the wall and, while Homily was making the tea, he tidied up the annex, stacking the ears of wheat alongside the boot, straightening the borrowing-bags, and generally seeing all was shipshape for the night. When he had finished he crossed to the hanging shelf and ran a loving hand along his neatly hanging row of tools. Just before they doused the light, he stood for a long time, deep in thought—his hand on an empty nail.

10

"Necessity hath no Law."
Brigham Young died, 1877

[Extract from Arrietty's Diary and
Proverb Book, August 29th]

They slept well and woke next morning bright and
early. The sun poured slantwise into the alcove and,
when Pod had unlaced it, into the neck of the boot.
For breakfast Arrietty gathered six wild strawberries
and Homily broke up some wheat grains with Pod's
small bell-clapper which, sprinkled with water, they
ate as cereal. "And, if you're still hungry, Arrietty,"
remarked Homily, "you can get yourself a nut."
(Arrietty was and did.)

The program for the day was arranged as follows:
Pod, in view of last night's happening, was to make
a solitary expedition across the field to the island
of trees in the center, in one last bid to find the
badger's set. Homily, because of her fear of open
spaces, would have to stay behind and Arrietty, Pod
said, must keep her company. "There's plenty of
jobs about the house," he told them. "To start with

you can weatherproof one of the borrowing-bags, rub it all over hard with a bit of candle, and it'll do for carting water. Then you can take the fretsaw and saw off a few hazelnuts for drinking out of and while you're about it you can gather a few extra nuts and store them in the annex, seeing as we don't have a spade. There's a nice bit o' horsehair I saw in the hedge going toward the stile, caught on a bramble bush: you can fetch a bit o' that along, if you feel like it, and I'll see about making a fishnet. And a bit more corn-crushing wouldn't come amiss. . . ."

"Oh, come on, Pod—" protested Homily. "Oblige you, we'd like to, but we're not slaves."

"Well," said Pod, gazing thoughtfully across the ocean of tussocky grass, "it'll take me pretty near all day—getting there, searching around, and getting back: I don't want you fretting . . ."

"I knew it would end like this," said Homily later, in a depressed voice, as she and Arrietty were waxing the borrowing-bag. "What did I tell you always, back home, when you wanted to emigrate? Didn't I tell you just how it would be—drafts, moths, worms, snakes and whatnot? And you saw how it was when it rained? What's it going to be like in winter? You tell me that. No one can say I'm not trying," she went on, "and no one won't hear a word of grumble pass my lips, but you mark my words, Arrietty, we won't none of us see another spring." And a round tear fell on the waxed cloth and rolled away like a marble.

"What with the ratcatcher," Arrietty pointed out, "we wouldn't have if we stayed back home."

"And I wouldn't be surprised," Homily persisted, "if that boy wasn't right. Remember what he said about the end of the race? Our time is come, I shouldn't wonder. If you ask me, we're dying out."

But she cheered up a bit when they took the bag down to the water to fill it up and a sliver of soap to wash with: the drowsy heat and the gentle stir of ripples past their landing stage of bark seemed always to calm her; and she even encouraged Arrietty to have a bath and let her splash about a little in the shallows. For a being so light the water was incredibly buoyant and it would not be very long, Arrietty felt, before she would learn to swim. Where she had used the soap the water went cloudy and softly translucent, the shifting color of moonstones.

After her bath Arrietty felt refreshed and left Homily in the annex to "get the tea" and went on up the hedge to collect the horsehair. Not that there was anything to "get," Homily thought irritably, setting out a few hips and haws, and some watercress, and cracking a couple of nuts with the bell-clapper.

The horsehair, caught on a bramble, was halfway up the hedge, but Arrietty, refreshed by her dip, was glad of a chance to climb. On the way down, seeking a foothold, she let out a tiny scream: her toes had touched, not the cool bark, but something soft and warm. She hung there, grasping the horsehair and staring through the leaves. All was still— nothing but tangled branches, flecked with sunlight. After a second or two, in which she hardly dared to breathe, a flicker of movement caught her eye as though the tip of a branch had swayed. Staring she saw, like a bunch of budding twigs, the shape of a brownish hand. It could not be a hand, of course, she told herself, but that's what it looked like, with tiny, callused fingers no larger than her own. Picking up courage, she touched it with her foot and the hand grasped her toes. Screaming and struggling, she lost her balance and came tumbling through the few remaining branches on to the dead leaves below. With her had fallen a small laughing creature no taller than herself. "That frighted you," it said.

Arrietty stared, breathing quickly. He had a brown face, black eyes, tousled dark hair and was dressed in what she guessed to be shabby moleskin, worn smooth side out: he seemed so soiled and earth-darkened that he matched not only the dead leaves into which they had fallen but the blackened branches as well. "Who are you?" she asked.

"Spiller," he said cheerfully, lying back on his elbows.

"You're filthy," remarked Arrietty disgustedly after a moment. She was still very angry.

"Maybe," he said.

"Where do you live?"

His dark eyes became sly and amused. "Here and there," he said, watching her closely.

"How old are you?"

"I don't know," he said.

"Are you a boy or grown-up?"

"I don't know," he said.

"Don't you ever wash?"

"No," he said.

"Well," said Arrietty, after an awkward silence, twisting the coarse strands of grayish horsehair about her wrist, "I'd better be going . . ."

"To that hole in the bank?" he asked—the hint of a jeer in his voice.

Arrietty looked startled. "Do you know it?" When he smiled, she noticed, his lips turned steeply upwards at the corners making his mouth a "V": it was the most teasing kind of smile she had ever seen.

"Haven't you ever seen a moth before?" he asked.

"You were watching last night?" exclaimed Arrietty.

"Were it private?" he asked.

"In a way: it's our home."

But he looked bored suddenly, turning his bright gaze away as though searching the more distant grasses. Arrietty opened her mouth to speak but he silenced her with a peremptory gesture, his eyes on the field below. Very curious, she watched him rise cautiously to his feet and then, in a single movement, spring to a branch above his head, reach for something out of sight and drop again to the ground. The object, she saw, was a taut, dark bow strung with gut and almost as tall as he was; in the other hand, he held an arrow.

Staring into the long grass, he laid the arrow to the bow, the gut twanged and the arrow was gone. There was a faint squeak.

"You've killed it," cried Arrietty, distressed.

"I meant to," he replied and sprang down the bank into the field. He made his way to the tussock of grass and returned after a moment with a dead field mouse swinging from his hand. "You got to eat," he explained.

Arrietty felt deeply shocked. She did not know quite why—at home, under the kitchen, they had always eaten meat; but borrowed meat from the kitchen upstairs: she had seen it raw but she had never seen it killed.

"We're vegetarians," she said primly. He took no notice: this was just a word to Spiller, one of the noises which people made with their mouths. "Do you want some meat?" he asked casually. "You can have a leg."

"I wouldn't touch it," cried Arrietty indignantly. She rose to her feet, brushing down her skirt. "Poor thing," she said, referring to the field mouse, "and I think you're horrid," she said, referring to him.

"Who isn't?" remarked Spiller, and reached above his head for his quiver.

"Let me look," begged Arrietty, turning back, suddenly curious.

He passed it to her: it was made, she saw, of a glove finger—the thickish leather of a country glove; the arrows were dry pine needles, tipped with blackthorn.

"How do you stick the thorns to the shaft?" she asked.

"Wild plum gum," replied Spiller.

"Are they poisoned?" asked Arrietty.

"No," said Spiller. "Fair's fair. Hit or miss. They got to eat—I got to eat. And I kill 'em quicker than an owl does. Nor I don't eat so many." It was quite a long speech for Spiller. He slung his quiver over his shoulder and turned away. "I'm going," he said.

Arrietty scrambled quickly down the bank. "So am I," she told him.

They walked along in the dry ditch together. Spiller, she noticed, as he walked glanced sharply about him: the bright black eyes were never still. Sometimes, at a slight rustle in grass or hedge, he would become motionless: there would be no tensing of muscles—he would just cease to move. On such occasions, Arrietty realized, he exactly matched his background. Once he dived into a clump of dead bracken and came out again with a struggling insect.

"Here you are," he said and Arrietty, staring, saw some kind of angry beetle.

"What is it?" she asked.

"A cricket. They're nice. Take it."

"To eat?" asked Arrietty, aghast.

"Eat? No. You take it home and keep it. Sings a treat," he added.

Arrietty hesitated. "You carry it," she said, without committing herself.

When they came abreast of the alcove, Arrietty looked up and saw that Homily, tired of waiting, had dozed off. She was sitting on the sunlit sand and had slumped against the boot.

"Mother—" she called softly from below and Homily woke at once. "Here's Spiller . . ." Arrietty went on, a trifle uncertainly.

"Here's what?" asked Homily, without interest. "Did you get the horsehair?"

Arrietty glancing sideways at Spiller saw that he was in one of his stillnesses and had become invisible. "It's my mother," she whispered. "Speak to her. Go on."

Homily, hearing a whisper, peered down, screwing her eyelids against the setting sun.

"What shall I say?" asked Spiller. Then, clearing his voice, he made an effort. "I got a cricket," he said. Homily screamed: it took her a moment to add the dun-colored patches together into the shapes of face, eyes and hands; it was to Homily as though the grass had spoken.

"What ever is it?" she gasped. "Oh, my goodness gracious, Arrietty, whatever have you got there?"

"It's a cricket," said Spiller again, but it was not to this insect Homily referred.

"It's Spiller," Arrietty repeated more loudly, and in an aside she whispered to Spiller, "Drop that dead thing and come on up. . . ."

Spiller not only dropped the field mouse but a fleeting echo of some dim, half-forgotten code must have flicked his memory, and he laid aside his bow as well. Unarmed, he climbed the bank.

Homily stared at Spiller rather rudely when he stepped onto the sandy platform before the boot. She moved right forward, keeping him at bay. "Good afternoon," she said coldly. It was as though she spoke from the threshold.

Spiller dropped the cricket and propelled it toward her with his toe. "Here you are," he said. Homily screamed again, very loudly and angrily, as the cricket scuttled, knee high, past her skirts and made for the darker shadow behind the boot. "It's a present, Mother," Arrietty explained indignantly. "It's a cricket: it sings—"

But Homily would not listen. "How dare you!

How dare you! How dare you! You naughty, dirty, unwashed boy." She was nearly in tears. "How could you? You go straight out of my house this minute. Lucky," she went on, "that my husband's not at home, nor my brother Hendreary neither. . . ."

"Uncle Hendreary—" began Arrietty, surprised, and, if looks could kill, Homily would have struck her dead.

"Take your beetle," Homily went on to Spiller, "and go! And never let me see you here again!" As Spiller hesitated, she added in a fury, "Do you hear what I say?"

Spiller threw a swift look toward the rear of the boot and a somewhat pathetic one toward Arrietty. "You can keep it," he said gruffly, and dived off down the bank.

"Oh, Mother—" exclaimed Arrietty reproachfully: she stared at the "tea" her mother had set out, and even the fact that her mother had filled the half hips with clover honey milked from the blooms, failed to interest her. "Poor Spiller! You were rude. . . ."

"Well, who is he? What does he want here? Where did you find him? Forcing his way on respectable people and flinging beetles about! Wouldn't be surprised if we all woke up one day with our throats cut. Did you see the dirt! Ingrained! I wouldn't be surprised if he hadn't left a flea—" and she seized the thistle-broom and briskly swept the spot where the miserable Spiller had placed his unwelcome feet. "I never had such an experience as this. Never! Not in all my born days. Now, that's the type," she concluded fiercely, "who would steal a hat pin!"

Secretly, Arrietty thought so, too, but she did not say so, using her tongue instead to lick a little of the honey out of the split rose hip. She also thought, as she savored the sun-warmed sweetness, that Spiller, the huntsman, would make better use of the hat pin than either her mother or father could. She wondered why he wanted the half nail scissor. "Have you had your tea?" she asked Homily after a moment.

"I've eaten a couple of wheat grains," admitted Homily in a martyred voice. "Now I must air the bedding."

Arrietty smiled, gazing out across the sunlit field. The bedding was one piece of sock—poor Homily with practically no housework had little on which to vent her energy. Well, now she'd had Spiller and it had done her good—her eyes looked brighter and her cheeks pinker. Idly, Arrietty watched a small bird picking its way amongst the grasses—no, it was too steady for a bird. "Here comes Papa," she said after a moment.

They ran down to meet him. "Well?" cried Homily eagerly, but as they drew closer, she saw by his face that the news he brought was bad. "You didn't find it?" she asked in a disappointed voice.

"I found it all right," said Pod.

"What's the matter then? Why do you look so down? You mean—they weren't there? You mean—they've left?"

"They've left, all right. Or been eaten." Pod stared unhappily.

"What can you mean, Pod?" stammered Homily.

"It's full o' foxes," he told them ponderously, his eyes still round with shock. "Smells awful . . ." he added after a moment.

11

"Misfortunes make us wise."
Sultan of Turkey deposed, 1876

[Extract from Arrietty's Diary and
Proverb Book, August 30th]

Homily carried on a bit that evening: it was
understandable—what were they faced with now?
This kind of Robinson Crusoe existence for the rest
of their lives? Raw food in the summer was bad
enough, but in the stark cold of winter, Homily
protested, it could not sustain life. Not that they
had the faintest chance of surviving the winter, anyway, without some form of heat. A bit of wax candle
would not last forever. Nor would their few wax
matches. And supposing they made a fire of sticks,
it would have to be colossal—an absolute confla-
gration it would appear to a borrower—to keep alight
at all. And the smoke of this, she pointed out, would
be seen for miles. No, she concluded gloomily, they
were in for it now and no two ways about it, as Pod
and Arrietty would see for themselves, poor things,
when the first frosts came.

It was the sight of Spiller perhaps which had shaken Homily, confirming her worst premonitions—uncouth, unwashed, dishonest, and ill-bred, that's what she summed him up to be, everything she most detested and feared. And this was the level (as she had often warned them back home) to which borrowers must sink if ever, for their sins, they attempted to live out-of-doors.

To make matters worse, they were awakened that night by a strange sound—a prolonged and maniac bellow, it sounded to Arrietty, as she lay there trembling—breath held and heart racing. "What was it?" she whispered to Pod when at last she dare speak.

The boot creaked as Pod sat up in bed: " 'Tis a donkey," he said, "but close." After a moment he added, "Funny—I ain't ever seen a donkey hereabouts."

"Nor I," whispered Arrietty. But she felt somehow relieved and was just preparing to settle down again when another sound, closer, caught her ear. "Listen!" she said sharply, sitting up.

"You don't want to lie awake listening," Pod grumbled, turning over and pulling after him an unfair share of the sock. "Not at night, you don't."

"It's in the annex," whispered Arrietty.

The boot creaked again as Pod sat up. "Keep

quiet, Pod, do," grumbled Homily, who had managed to doze off.

"Quiet yourself," said Pod, trying to concentrate. It was a small whirring sound he heard, very regular. "You're right," he breathed to Arrietty, "it's in the annex." He threw off the sock which Homily clutched at angrily, pulling it back about her shoulders. "I'm going out," he said.

"No, Pod, you don't!" implored Homily huskily. "We're all right here, laced up. Stay quiet. . . ."

"No, Homily, I got to see." He felt his way along the ankle of the boot. "Stay quiet, the two of you. I won't be long."

"Oh, dear," exclaimed Homily in a scared voice. "Then take the hat pin," she implored nervously as she saw him begin to unthread the laces. Arrietty, watching, saw the boot fall open and her father's head and shoulders appear suddenly against the night sky: there was a scrabbling, a rustling and a skittering—and Pod's voice shouting, "Dang you . . . dang you . . . dang you!" Then there was silence.

Arrietty crept along the ankle of the boot and put her head out into the air: their cave was filled with bright moonlight, and every object could be plainly seen. Arrietty stepped out and looked about her. A silvery Pod stood on the lip of the alcove, staring down at the moon-drenched field.

"What was it?" called Homily from the depths of the boot.

"Danged field mice," called Pod, "been at the corn."

And Arrietty saw in that pale, friendly light that the sandy floor of the annex was strewn with empty husks.

"Well, that's that," said Pod, turning back and kicking the scattered husks. "Better get the thistle," he added, "and sweep up the mess."

Arrietty did so, almost dancing. Enchanted, she felt, by this friendly radiance which lent an unfamiliar magic to even the most matter-of-fact objects such as Pod's bell-clapper hanging from its nail and the whitened stitching on the boot. When she had made three neat piles of husks, she joined Pod at the lip of the alcove and they sat silent for a while on the still warm sand, listening to the night.

An owl called from the spinney beside the brook—a fluting, musical note which was answered, at great distance, by a note as haunting in a slightly higher key: weaving a shuttle of sound back and forth across the sleeping pasture, linking the sea of moonlight and the velvet shadowed woods.

Whatever the danger, Arrietty thought, sitting there at peace beside her father, whatever the difficulty, I still am glad we came.

"What we need in this place," said Pod at last, breaking the long silence, "is some kind of tin."

"Tin?" repeated Arrietty vaguely, not sure she had understood.

"Or a couple of tins. A cocoa tin would do. Or one of them they use for 'baccy." He was silent awhile, and then he added, "That pit we dug weren't deep enough: bet them danged field mice have been at the nuts."

"Couldn't you learn to shoot a bow and arrow?" asked Arrietty after a moment.

"Whatever for?" asked Pod.

Arrietty hesitated. Then, all in a breath, she told him about Spiller; the well-sprung bow, the thorn-tipped, deadly arrows. And she described how

Spiller had been watching them from the darkness when they played out their scene with the moth on the stage of the lighted alcove.

"I don't like that," said Pod after a moment's thought, "not neighbors watching, I don't like. Can't have that, you know. Not by night nor by day neither; it ain't healthy, if you get my meaning."

Arrietty did get his meaning. "What we want here is some kind of shutter or door. A piece of chicken wire might do. Or that cheese grater, perhaps—the one we had at home. It would have to be something that lets the light in, I mean," she went on. "We can't go back to living in the dark."

"I got an idea," said Pod suddenly. He stood up and, turning about, craned his neck upwards to the overhang above. The slender sapling, silvery with moonlight, leaned above the bank. Pod stared a moment at the leaves against the sky as though calculating distances; then, looking down, he kicked about the sand with his feet.

"What is it?" whispered Arrietty, thinking he had lost something.

"Ah—" said Pod, in a pleased voice and went down on his knees. "This 'ould do." And he shoveled about with his hands, uncovering after a moment a snaking loop of tough root, seemingly endless. "Yes," he repeated. "This'll do fine."

"What for?" asked Arrietty, wildly curious.

"Get me the twine," said Pod. "There on that shelf, where the tools are—"

Arrietty, standing on tiptoe, reached her hand into the sandy recess and found the ball of twine.

"Give it here," said Pod, "and get me the bell-clapper."

Arrietty watched her father tie a length of twine on to the bell-clapper and, balancing a little perilously on the very edge of their terrace, take careful aim and, with a violent effort, fling the clapper up into the branches above: it caught hold, like an anchor, among a network of twigs.

"Now, come on," said Pod to Arrietty, breathing steadily. "Take hold and pull. Gently does it . . . steady now. Gently . . . gently . . ." And leaning together, their full weight on the twine, hand over hand they drew down the stooping branch. The alcove became dark suddenly with broken shadow, cut and trembling with filtered moonlight.

"Hold on," panted Pod, guiding the twine to the loop of root, "while I make her fast." He gave a grunt. "There," he said and stood up, rubbing the strain out of his hands (he was flecked all over, Arrietty noticed, with blobs of silver). "Get me the half scissor. Dang it, I forgot—the fretsaw will do."

It was hard to lay hands on the fretsaw in this

1 3 1

sudden darkness, but at last she found it and Pod cut his halliard. "There," he said again in a satisfied voice. "She's fast—and we're covered. How's that for an idea? You can let her up or down, depending on what goes on, wind, weather and all the rest of it. . . ."

He removed the bell-clapper and made the twine fast to the main branch. "Won't keep the field mice out, nor them kind of cattle—but," he gave a satisfied laugh, "there won't be no more watching."

"It's wonderful," said Arrietty, her face among the leaves, "—and we can still see out."

"That's the idea," said Pod. "Come on now: time we got back to bed!"

As they felt their way toward the mouth of the boot, Pod tripped against a pile of wheat husks and stumbled, coughing, into their dusty scatter. As he stood up and brushed himself down, he remarked thoughtfully, "Spiller—you said his name was?" He was silent a moment and then added thoughtfully, "There's a lot worse food, when you come to think of it, than a piping-hot, savory stew made of corn-fed field mouse."

12

"Better suffer ill, than do ill."
Disastrous Earthquake at Charleston, U.S., 1866

[Extract from Arrietty's Diary and
Proverb Book, August 31st]

Homily was in a worried mood next morning. "What's all this?" she grumbled when, a little tousled, she crept out of the boot and saw that the alcove was filled with a greenish, underwater light.

"Oh, Mother," exclaimed Arrietty reproachfully. "It's lovely!" A faint breeze stirred the clustered leaves which, parting and closing, let pass bright spears and arrows of dancing light—a delightful blend of mystery and gaiety (or so it seemed to Arrietty). "Don't you see," she went on as its inventor preserved a proud silence, "Papa made it: it's quick cover—lets in the light but keeps out the rain; and we can see out but they can't see in."

"Who's they?" asked Homily.

"Anything . . . anybody passing. Spiller," she added on a gleam of inspiration.

Homily relented. "H'mm," she vouchsafed in a noncommittal tone, but she examined the uncovered root in the floor, noted the clove hitch, and ran a thoughtful finger down the taut twine.

"The thing to remember," Pod explained earnestly, aware of her tardy approval, "is—when you let her go—keep hold of the halliard: you don't want this here halliard ever to leave the root. See what I mean?"

Homily saw. "But you don't want to waste the sunshine," she pointed out, "not while it's summer, you don't. Soon it will be—" she shuddered slightly and tightened her lips, unable to say the word.

"Well, winter ain't here yet," exclaimed Pod lightly. "Sufficient unto the day, as they say—" He was busy with the halliard. "Here you are—up she goes!" and, as the twine ran squeaking under the root, the leaves flew up out of sight and the alcove leaped into light.

"See what I mean?" said Pod again, in a satisfied voice.

During breakfast the donkey brayed again, loud and long, and was answered almost at once by the neigh of a horse.

"I don't like it," said Homily suddenly, setting down her half hazel shell of honey and water. Even as she spoke, a dog yelped—too close for comfort. Homily started—and over went the honey and water, a dark stain on the sandy floor. "Me nerves is all pieces—" Homily wailed, then clapped her hands to her temples and looked from side to side with wild eyes.

"It's nothing, Mother," Arrietty explained, irritated. "There's a lane just below the spinney: I saw it from the top of the hedge. It's people passing, that's all. They're bound to pass sometimes. . . ."

"That's right," agreed Pod. "You don't want to worry. You eat up your grain—"

Homily stared distastefully at the bitten-into grain of corn (dry and hard as a breakfast roll three days after a picnic). "Me teeth ain't up to it," she said unhappily.

"According to Arrietty," explained Pod, holding up the spread fingers of his left hand and knocking each back in turn, "between us and that lane we got five barriers—the stream down at the corner— one; them posts with rusty wire across the stream— two; a fair-sized wood—three; another hedge—four; and a bit o' rough grazing ground—five." He turned to Arrietty. "Ain't that right, lass? You been up the hedge?"

Arrietty agreed. "But that bit of grazing ground belongs to the lane—a kind of grass verge."

"There you are then," exclaimed Pod triumphantly, slapping Homily on the back. "Common land! And someone's tethered a donkey there. What's wrong with that? Donkeys don't eat you—no more don't horses."

"A dog might," said Homily. "I heard a dog."

"And what of it?" exclaimed Pod. "It wasn't the first time and it won't be the last. When I was a lad, down at the big house, the place was awash with setters, as you might say. Dogs is all right: you can talk to dogs."

Homily was silent a moment, rolling the wheat grain backwards and forwards on the flat piece of slate which they used as a table.

"It's no good," she said at last.

"What's no good?" asked Pod, dismayed.

"Going on like this," said Homily. "We got to do something before winter."

"Well, we are doing something, aren't we?" said Pod. He nodded toward Arrietty. "Like it says in her book—Rome weren't built in a day."

"Find some kind of human habitation," went on Homily, "that's what we've got to do—where there's fires and pickings and proper sort of cover." She hesitated. "Or," she went on in a set determined voice, "we got to go back home."

There was a stunned silence. "We got to do what?" asked Pod weakly, when he could find his voice; and Arrietty deeply upset, breathed, "Oh, Mother—"

"You heard me, Pod," said Homily. "All these hips and haws and watercress and dogs barking and foxes in the badger's set and creeping in the night and stealing and rain coming up and nothing to cook on. You see what I mean? Back home, in the big house, it wouldn't take us no time to put a few partitions up and get kind of straight again under the kitchen. We did it once, that time the boiler burst: we can do it again."

Pod stared across at her and when he spoke he spoke with the utmost gravity. "You don't know what you're saying, Homily. It's not just that they'll be waiting for us; that they've got the cat; set traps; laid down poison and all that caper. It's just that you don't *go back*, Homily, not once you've come out, you don't. And we ain't *got* a home. That's all over and done with. Like it or not, we got to go on now. See what I mean?" When Homily did not reply, he turned his grave face to Arrietty.

"I'm not saying we're not up against it; we are— right up against it. More than I like to let on. And if we don't stick together, we're finished—see? And it will be the end—like you once said, Arrietty— the end of our race! Never let me hear another word from either one of you, you or your mother, about"—with great solemnity he slightly raised his voice, stressing each word — "going back any- where—let alone under the floor!"

They were very impressed; they both stared back at him unable, for the moment, to speak.

"Understand?" asked Pod sternly.

"Yes, Papa," whispered Arrietty; and Homily swallowed, nodding her head.

"That's right," Pod told them more gently. "Like it says in your book, Arrietty, 'A Word is enough to the Wise.' "

"Now get me the horsehair," he went on more jovially. "It's a nice day. And while you two clear breakfast, I'll start on the fishnet. How's that?" Homily nodded again. She did not even ask him, as on any other occasion she would have immediately, how, when they had caught the fish, he proposed that they should cook it. "There's a nice lot of dry bark about. Do fine," said Pod, "for floats."

But Pod, though good at knots, had quite a bit of trouble with the horsehair: the long tail-strands were springy and would slide from the eye of the needle. When the chores were done, however, and Arrietty sent off to the brook with two borrowing- bags—the waxed one for water and the other for bark—Homily came to Pod's rescue and, working together, they evolved a close mesh on the spider-

web principle, based on Homily's knowledge of tat-
ting.

"What about this Spiller?" Pod asked uneasily
after a while, as he sat beside Homily, watching her
fingers.

Homily snorted, busy with her knots. "Don't talk
to me of that one—" she said after a moment.

"Is he a borrower or what?" asked Pod.

"I don't know what he is," cried Homily, "and
what's more, I don't care neither. Threw a beetle at
me, that's all I know. And stole the pin and our nail
scissor."

"You know that for sure?" asked Pod, on a rising
note.

"Sure as I'm sitting here," said Homily. "You
ain't seen him."

Pod was silent a moment. "I'd like to meet him,"
he said after a while, staring out across the sunlit
field.

The net grew apace and the time went by almost
without their noticing. Once when, each taking an
end, they held the work out for inspection, a grasshopper sprang from the bank below, bulletlike, into
the meshes; and it was only after—with infinite care
for the net—they had freed the struggling creature
that Homily thought of luncheon.

"Goodness," she cried, staring across the field,

"look at them shadows! Must be after two. What can have happened to Arrietty?"

"Playing down there with the water, I shouldn't wonder," said Pod.

"Didn't you tell her 'there and back and no dawdling'?"

"She knows not to dawdle," said Pod.

"That's where you're wrong, Pod, with Arrietty. With Arrietty you got to say it every time!"

"She's going on for fourteen now," said Pod.

"No matter," Homily told him, rising to her feet. "She's young for her age. You always got to tell her, else she'll make excuses."

Homily folded up the net, brushed herself down and bustled across the annex to the shelf above the tool rack.

"You hungry, Pod?" It was a rhetorical question: they were always hungry, all of them, every hour of the day. Even after meals, they were hungry.

"What is there?" he asked.

"There's a bunch of haws, a couple of nuts and a mildewed blackberry."

Pod sighed. "All right," he said.

"But which?" asked Homily.

"The nut's more filling," said Pod.

"But what can I do, Pod?" cried Homily unhappily. "Any suggestions? Do you want to go and pick us a couple of wild strawberries?"

"That's an idea," said Pod, and he moved toward the bank.

"But you got to look careful," Homily told him. "They've got a bit scarce now. Something's been at them. Birds maybe. Or," she added bitterly, "more likely that Spiller."

"Listen!" cried Pod, raising a warning hand. He stood quite still at the edge of their cave, staring away to his left.

"What was it?" whispered Homily, after a moment.

"Voices," said Pod.

"What kind of voices?"

"Human," said Pod.

"Oh, my—" whispered Homily fearfully.

"Quiet," said Pod.

They stood quite still, ears attuned. There was a faint hum of insects from the grasses below and the buzzing of a fly which had blundered into the alcove. It flew jerkily about between them and settled greedily at last on the sandy floor where at breakfast Homily had spilled the honey. Then suddenly, uncomfortably close, they heard a different sound, a sound which drove the color from their

cheeks and which filled their hearts with dread—
and it was, on the face of it, a cheerful sort of sound:
the sound of a human laugh.

Neither moved: frozen, they stood—pale and
tense with listening. There was a pause and, nearer
now, a man's voice cursed—one short, sharp word
and, immediately after, they heard the yelp of a
dog.

Pod stooped; swiftly with a jerk of the wrist, he
released the halliard and, hand over steady hand,
he pulled on the swaying tree: this time, he used
extra strength, drawing the branches lower and closer
until he had stuffed the mouth of their cave with a
close-knit network of twigs.

"There," he gasped, breathing hard. "Take some
getting through, that will."

Homily, bewildered by the dappled half-light,
could not make out his expression, but somehow
she sensed his calm. "Will it look all right from
outside?" she asked evenly, matching her tone to
his.

"Should do," said Pod. He went up to the leaves
and peered out between them, and with steady hands
and sure grip tried the set of the branches. "Now,"
he said, stepping back and drawing a deep breath,
"hand me that other hat pin."

Then it was that a strange thing happened: Pod

put out his hand—and there at once was the hat pin, but it had been put in his grasp too quietly and too immediately to have been put there by Homily: a shadowy third shared their dim-lit cavern, a dun-colored creature of invisible stillness. And the hat pin was the hat pin they had lost.

"Spiller!" gasped Homily hoarsely.

13

"Meat is much, but manners are more."
Louis XIV of France died, 1715

[Extract from Arrietty's Diary and
Proverb Book, September 1st]

He must have slid in with the lowering of the leaves—a shadow among shadows. Now she could see the blob of face, the tangled thatch of hair and that he carried two borrowing-bags, one empty and one full. And the bags, Homily realized with a sinking of the heart, were the bags which, that morning, she had handed to Arrietty.

"What have you done with her?" Homily cried, distraught. "What have you done with Arrietty?"

Spiller jerked his head toward the back of the alcove. "She's coming up over yon field," he said and his face remained quite expressionless. "I floated her off down the current," he added carelessly. Homily turned wild eyes toward the back of the alcove as though she might see through the sandy walls and into the field beyond: it was the field through which they had traipsed on the day of their escape.

"You what?" exclaimed Pod.

"Floated her off down the river," said Spiller, "in half of a soap box," he explained irritably, as though Pod were being dense.

Pod opened his mouth to reply—then, staring, remained silent: there was a sound of running footsteps in the ditch below; as they came abreast of the alcove and thundered past outside, the whole of the bank seemed to tremble and the bell-clapper fell off its nail—they heard the steady rasp of men's harsh breathing and the panting of a dog.

"It's all right," said Spiller, after a tense pause. "They cut off left, and across. Gypsies," he added tersely, "out rabbiting."

"Gypsies?" echoed Pod dully, and he wiped his brow with his sleeve.

"That's right," said Spiller. "Down there by the lane; coupla caravans."

"Gypsies . . ." breathed Homily in a blank kind of wonderment, and for a moment she was silent—her breath held and her mouth open, listening.

"It's all right," said Spiller, listening, too. "They gone across now, alongside the cornfield."

"And what's this now about Arrietty?" stammered Pod.

"I told you," said Spiller.

"Something about a soap dish?"

"Is she all right?" implored Homily, interrupting. "Is she safe? Tell us that—"

"She's safe," said Spiller. "I told you. Box, not dish," he corrected and glanced interestedly about the alcove. "I slept in that boot once," he announced conversationally, nodding his head toward it.

Homily repressed a shudder. "Never mind that now," she said, hurriedly dismissing the subject. "You go on and tell us about Arrietty. This soap dish or box or whatever it was. Tell us just what happened."

It was difficult to piece the story together from Spiller's terse sentences, but at last some coherence emerged. Spiller, it seemed, owned a boat—the bottom half of an aluminum soap case, slightly dented; in this, standing up, he would propel himself about the stream. Spiller had a summer camp, or hunting lodge, in the sloping field behind—an old blackened teakettle it was—wedged sideways in the silt of the stream (he had several of these bases it appeared, of which, at some time, the boot had been one)—and he would borrow from the caravans, transporting the loot by water; this boat gave him a speedy getaway, and one which left no scent. Coming up against the current was slower, Spiller explained, and for this he was grateful for the hat pin which not only served as a sharp and pliable punt-pole, but as a harpoon as well. He became so lyrical about the hat pin, that Pod and Homily began to feel quite pleased with themselves as though, out of the kindness of their hearts, they had achieved some benevolent gesture. Pod longed to ask to what use Spiller had put the half nail scissor but could not bring himself to do so, fearing to strike a discordant note in a state of innocent joy.

On this particular afternoon, it seemed, Spiller had been transporting two lumps of sugar, a twist of tea, three leaden hair-curlers and one of those plain gold earrings for pierced ears, known as sleepers, across the wider part of the brook where, pond-like, it spread into their field, when (he told them) he had seen Arrietty at the water's edge, barefoot in the warm mud, playing some kind of game. She had a quill-like leaf of bulrush in her hand and seemed to be stalking frogs. She would steal up behind her prey, where innocently it sat basking in the sun, and—when she was close enough—she would tap the dozing creature smartly in the small of its back with her swaying length of wand. There would then be a croak, a plop, a splash—and it was one up to Arrietty. Sometimes she was seen approaching—then, of course, it was one up to the frog. She challenged Spiller to a match, completely unaware, he said, that she had another interested spectator—the Gypsies' dog, a kind of mongrel greyhound, which stared with avid eyes from the woodland edge of the pond. Nor, he added, had she heard the crackling in the underbrush which meant that its masters were close behind.

Spiller, it seemed, had just had time to leap ashore, push Arrietty into the shallow soap box and, with a few hurried directions about the whereabouts of the kettle, shove her off downstream.

"But will she ever find it?" gasped Homily. "The kettle, I mean?"

"Couldn't miss it," said Spiller, and went on to explain that the current fetched up close against the spout, in a feathery pileup of broken ripples—and there the soap box always stuck. "All she got to do," he pointed out, "is make fast, tip the stuff out and walk on back up."

"Along the ridge of the gas pipe?" asked Pod. Spiller threw him a startled glance, shrewd but somehow closed. "She could do," he said shortly.

"Half a soap box . . ." murmured Homily wonderingly, trying to picture it. ". . . hope she'll be all right."

"She'll be all right," said Spiller, "and there b'ain't no scent on the water."

"Why didn't you get in, too," asked Pod, "and go along with her, like?"

Spiller looked faintly uncomfortable. He rubbed his dark hand on the back of his moleskin trousers; he frowned slightly, glancing at the ceiling. "There b'ain't room for two," he said at last; "not with cargo."

"You could have tipped the cargo out," said Pod.

Spiller frowned more deeply as though the subject bored him. "Maybe," he said.

"I mean," Pod pointed out, "there you were, weren't you? Out in the open, left without cover. What's a bit of cargo compared to that?"

"Yes," said Spiller and added uncomfortably, referring to his boat, "she's shallow—you ain't seen her: there b'ain't room for two."

"Oh, Pod—" cried Homily, suddenly emotional.

"Now what?" asked Pod.

"This boy," went on Homily in ringing tones, "this— Well, anyway, there he stands!" and she threw out an arm toward Spiller.

Pod glanced at Spiller: yes, indeed, there he stood, very embarrassed and indescribably grubby.

"He saved her life," went on Homily, throaty with gratitude, "at the expense of his own!"

"Not expense," Pod pointed out after a moment,

staring thoughtfully at Spiller. "I mean he's here, isn't he?" And added reasonably in surprised afterthought, "And she's not!"

"She will be," said Homily, suddenly confident. "You'll see; everything's all right. And he's welcome to the hat pin. This boy's a hero." Suddenly herself again, she began to bustle about. "Now you sit here, Spiller," she urged him hospitably, "and rest yourself. It's a long pull up from the water. What'll you take? Could you do with a nice half of rose hip filled with something or other? We haven't much," she explained with a nervous laugh. "We're newcomers, you see. . . ."

Spiller put a grubby hand into a deep pocket. "I got this," he said and threw down a sizable piece of something heavy which bounced juicily as it hit the slate table. Homily moved forward; curiously, she stooped. "What is it?" she asked in an awed voice. But even as she spoke she knew: a faint gamy odor rose to her nostrils—gamy but deliciously savory, and for one fleeting, glorious second she felt almost faint with greed: it was a roast haunch of—

"Meat," said Spiller.

"What kind of meat?" asked Pod: he, too, looked rather glassy-eyed—an exclusive diet of hips and haws might be non-acid-forming, but it certainly left corners.

"Don't tell me," Homily protested, clapping her hands to her ears. And, as they turned towards her, surprised, she looked apologetic but added eagerly, "Let's just eat it, shall we?"

They fell to, slicing it up with the sliver of razor-blade. Spiller looked on surprised: surfeited with regular protein, he was not feeling particularly hungry. "Lay a little by for Arrietty," Homily kept saying and every now and again she remembered her manners and would press Spiller to eat.

Pod, very curious, kept throwing out feelers. "Too big for field mouse," he would say, chewing thoughtfully, "yet too small for rabbit. You couldn't eat stoat. . . . Might be a bird, of course?"

And Homily, in a pained voice, would cry, "Please, Pod—" and would turn coyly to Spiller. "All *I* want to know is how Spiller cooks it. It's delicious and hung just right."

But Spiller would not be drawn. "It's easy," he admitted once to Homily's bewilderment: how could it be "easy" out here in a grateless wilderness devoid of coke or coal? And, natural gratitude apart, she made more and more fuss of Spiller: she had liked him, she was convinced now, from the first.

Arrietty returned in the middle of this feast. She staggered a little when she had pushed her way through the tight-packed screen of leaves, swayed on her two feet, and sat down rather suddenly in the middle of the floor.

Homily was all concern. "What have they done to you, Arrietty? What's the matter? Are you hurt?"

Arrietty shook her head. "Seasick," she said weakly. "My head's all awhirl." She glanced reproachfully across at Spiller. "You spun me out in the current," she told him accusingly. "The thing went round and round and round and round and round and round and—"

"Now, that's enough, Arrietty," interrupted Homily, "or you'll have us all whirling. Spiller was very kind. You should be grateful. He gave his life for yours—"

"He didn't give his life," explained Pod again, slightly irritated.

But Homily took no notice. "And then came on up here with the borrowing-bags to say you were all right. You should thank him."

"Thank you, Spiller," said Arrietty, politely but wanly, looking up from her place on the floor.

"Now get up," said Homily, "that's a good girl. And come to the table. Not had a bite since breakfast—that's all that's the matter with you: we've saved you a nice piece of meat. . . ."

"A nice piece of what?" asked Arrietty in a dazed voice, not believing her ears.

"Meat," said Homily firmly, without looking at her.

Arrietty jumped up and came across to the table; she stared blankly down at the neat brown slices. "But I thought we were vegetarians. . . ." After a moment she raised her eyes to Spiller: there was a question in them. "Is it—?" she began, unhappily.

Spiller shook his head quickly; it was a firm negative and settled her misgivings. "We never ask," put in Homily sharply, tightening her lips and creating a precedent. "Let's just call it a bit of what the Gypsies caught and leave it at that."

"Not leave it . . ." murmured Arrietty dreamily: quite recovered she seemed suddenly: and arranging her skirts she joined them at the low table round which they sat picnic-wise on the floor. Tentatively she took up a slice in two fingers, took a cautious bite, then closed her eyes and almost shuddered, so welcome and downright was the flavor. "*Did* the Gypsies catch it?" she asked incredulously.

"No," said Pod. "Spiller did."

"I thought so," Arrietty said. "Thank you, Spiller," she added. And this time, her voice sounded heartfelt—alive and ringing with proper gratitude.

14

"Pull gently on a weak rope."
First Balloon Ascent in England, 1784

[Extract from Arrietty's Diary and
Proverb Book, September 15th]

Meals became different after that—different and
better—and this had something to do, Arrietty decided, with their stolen half nail scissor. Stolen? An
unpleasant-sounding word, seldom applied to a borrower. "But what else can you call it?" Homily wailed
as she sat one morning on the edge of the alcove
while Pod sewed a patch on her shoe, "or expect,
even, of a poor, homeless, ignorant boy dragged up,
as they say, in the gutter. . . ."

"Ditch, you mean," put in Arrietty drowsily, who
was lying below on the bank.

"I mean gutter," repeated Homily, but she looked
a little startled: she had not known Arrietty was near.
"It's a manner of speaking. No," she went on primly,
adjusting the hem of her skirt to hide her stockinged
foot (there was a slight hole, she had noticed, in the
toe), "you can't blame the lad. I mean, with that

sort of background, what could he learn about ethics?"

"About whatticks?" asked Pod. Homily, poor ignorant soul, occasionally hit on a word which surprised him and, what surprised him still more, sometimes she hit on its meaning.

"Ethics," repeated Homily coolly and with perfect confidence. "You know what ethics are, don't you?"

"No, I don't," Pod admitted simply, sewing away on his patch. "Sounds to me like something you pick up in the long grass."

"Them's ticks," said Homily.

"Or," Pod went on, smoothing the neat join with a licked thumb, "that thing that horses get from drinking too quick."

"It's funny . . ." mused Arrietty, "that you can't have just one."

"One what?" asked Homily sharply.

"One ethic," said Arrietty.

"That's where you're wrong," snapped Homily. "As a matter of fact there is only one. And Spiller's never learned it. One day," she went on, "I'm going to have a nice, quiet, friendly talk with that poor lad. . . ."

"What about?" asked Arrietty.

Homily ignored the question: she had composed

her face to a certain kind of expression and was not going to change it. " 'Spiller,' I'll say, 'you never had a mother—' "

"How do you know he never had a mother?" asked Pod. "He must have had," he added reasonably after a moment's reflection.

"Yes," put in Arrietty, "he did have a mother. That's how he knows his name."

"How?" asked Homily, suddenly curious.

"Because his mother told him, of course! Spiller's his surname. His first name's Dreadful."

There was a pause.

"What is it?" asked Homily then, in an awed voice.

"Dreadful!"

"Never mind," snapped Homily. "Tell us: we're not children."

"That's his name: Dreadful Spiller. He remembers his mother saying it one day, at table: 'A Dreadful Spiller, that's what you are,' she said, 'aren't you?' It's about all he does remember about his mother."

"All right," said Homily, after a moment, composing her features back to gentle tolerance. "Then I'll say to him (she smiled her sad smile), 'Dreadful,' I'll say, 'dear boy, my poor orphan lad—' "

"How do you know he's orphaned?" interrupted

Pod. "Have you ever asked him if he's orphaned?"

"You can't ask Spiller things," put in Arrietty quickly. "Some ones he tells you, but you can't ask him. Remember when you tried to find out how he did the cooking? He didn't come back for two days."

"That's right," agreed Pod glumly. "Couple o' days without meat. We don't want that again in a hurry. Look here, Homily," he went on, turning suddenly toward her, "better leave Spiller alone."

"It's for his own good," protested Homily angrily, "and it's *telling*, not *asking*! I was only going to say—(again she smiled her smile) 'Spiller, my poor lad . . .' or 'Dreadful' or whatever his name is—"

"You can't call him Dreadful, Mother," put in Arrietty, "not unless he asks you—"

"Well, 'Spiller' then"—Homily threw up her eyes—"but I got to tell him."

"Tell him what?" asked Pod, irritated.

"This *ethic*!" Homily almost shouted. "This what we all been brought up on! That you don't never borrow from a borrower!"

Impatiently Pod snapped off his thread. "He knows that," he said. He handed the shoe to Homily. "Here, you, put it on."

"Then what about the hat pin?" persisted Homily.

"He give it back," Pod said.

"He didn't give back the nail scissor!"

"He skins the game with it," said Arrietty quickly. "And we get the meat."

"Skins the game?" pondered Homily. "Well, I never. . . ."

"That's right," agreed Pod, "and cuts it up. See what I mean, Homily?" He rose to his feet. "Better leave well alone."

Homily was struggling absentmindedly with the laces of her shoe. "Wonder how he does cook?" she mused aloud after a moment.

"Wonder away," said Pod: he crossed to the shelf to replace his tools. "No harm in that, so long as you don't ask."

"Poor orphaned lad . . ." said Homily again: she spoke quite lightly, but her eye was thoughtful.

15

"No joy without alloy."
Columbus discovered New World, 1492

[Extract from Arrietty's Diary and
Proverb Book, October 12th]

The next six weeks, according to Tom Goodenough,
were the happiest Arrietty ever spent out-of-doors.
Not that they could be called halcyon exactly: they
ran, of course, the usual gamut of English summer
weather—days when the fields were drowned in opal
mist and spiders' webs hung jeweled in the hedges:
days of breathless heat and stifling closeness; thun-
dery days with once a searing strike of lightning
across the woods when Homily, terrified, had buried
the razor blade saying that "steel attracts"; and one
whole week of dismal, steady rain with scarcely a
letup, when the ditch below their bank became a
roaring cataract on which Spiller, guiding his tin
soap case with uncanny speed and skill, intrepidly
shot the rapids; during this week, Homily and Arrietty were kept housebound in case, Pod told them,
they should slip on the mud and fall in: it would be
no joke, he explained, to be swept along down the

ditch to the swollen stream at the corner and on and on through the lower fields until they met the river and eventually, he concluded, be carried out to sea.

"Why not say 'across to America' and have done with it?" Homily had remarked tartly, remembering Arrietty's *Gazetteer of the World*. But she got ahead with her winter knitting, saw the men had hot drinks and dried out poor Spiller's clothes over the candle while he huddled naked, but clean for once, in the boot. The rain never actually beat into the alcove but there was an unpleasant dampness all over everything, white mildew on the leather of the boot, and, once, a sudden crop of yellow toadstools where none had been before. Another morning, when Homily crept forth shivering to get breakfast, a silvery track of slime wound ribbonlike across the floor and, putting her hand in the tool shelf for the matches, she gave a startled scream—stuffed, the shelf was, and flowing over with a heaving mass of slug. A slug that size cannot be easily tackled by a borrower, but luckily this one shrank up and feigned dead: once they had prized it out of its close-fitting retreat, they could bowl it over across the sandy floor and roll it away down to the bank.

After this, toward the end of October, there did come some halcyon days—about ten of them: sun and butterflies and drowsy heat; and a second burst of wildflowers. There was no end to Arrietty's amusements out-of-doors. She would climb down the bank, across the ditch and into the long grass and, stretched between the stems, would lie there watching. Once she became used to the habits of the insects, she no longer feared them: her world, she realized, was not their world and for them hers had little interest; except, perhaps for that buglike horror (an ethic to Pod) which, crawling sluggishly across bare skin would bury its head and cling.

Grasshoppers would alight like prehistoric birds on the grasses above her head; strange, armor-plated creatures, but utterly harmless to such as she. The grass stems would sway wildly beneath their sudden weight and Arrietty, lying watchful below, would note the machinelike slicing of the mandibles as the grasshopper munched its fill.

Bees, to Arrietty, were as big as birds are to humans; and if honeybees were pigeon-sized, a bumblebee in weight and girth could be compared to a turkey. These, too, she found, if unprovoked, were harmless. A quivering bumblebee, feeding greedily on clover, became strangely still all at once when, with gentle fingers, she stroked his fur. Benignity met with benignity: and anger, she found, was only roused through fear. Once she was nearly stung when, to tease it, she imprisoned a bee in that bloom called wild snapdragon by closing the lip with her hands. The trapped bee buzzed like a dynamo and stung, not Arrietty this time, but the enclosing calyx of the flower.

A good deal of time she would spend by the water—paddling, watching, learning to float. The frogs fought shy of her: at Arrietty's approach, they would plop away with bored bleats of distaste, their bulging eyes resigned but nervous; "Look where it comes again . . ."* they seemed to croak.

After bathing, before putting on her clothes, sometimes, she would dress up: a skirt of violet leaves, stalks uppermost, secured about the waist with a twist of faded columbine and, aping the fairies, a foxglove bell for a hat. This, Arrietty thought as she stared at her bright reflection in the stagnant water of a hoof crater, might look all right on gnomes, elves, brownies, pixies and whatnot, but she had to admit that it looked pretty silly on a common-or-garden borrower: for one thing, if the lip fitted the circumference of her head, the whole thing stood up too high like some kind of pinkish sausage or a very drawn-out chef's cap. Yet if, on the other hand, the lip of the bell flowed out generously in a gentle,

---

*"Tom Thumb Edition of Shakespeare's Tragedies, with foreword on the Author."

more hatlike curve, the whole contraption slid down past her face to rest on her shoulders in a Ku Klux Klan effect.

And to get hold of these bells at all was not easy: foxglove plants were high. Fairies, Arrietty supposed, just flew up to them with raised chins and neatly pointed toes, trailing a wisp of gauze. Fairies did everything so gracefully: Arrietty, poor girl, had to hook down the plant with a forked stick and sit on it as heavily as she could while she plucked any bells within reach. Sometimes the plant would escape her and fly up again. But usually, by shifting her weight along the stalk, she would manage to get five or six bells—sufficient anyway to try some out for size.

Spiller, gliding by in his cleverly loaded boat, would stare with some surprise: he was not altogether approving of Arrietty's games. Having spent all his life out-of-doors, fending for himself against nature, he had no picture of what such freedom could mean to one who had spent her childhood under a kitchen floor. Frogs were just meat to Spiller; grass was "cover"; and insects a nuisance, especially gnats; water was there to drink, not to splash in; and streams were highways which held fish. Spiller, poor harried creature, had never had time to play.

But he was a fearless borrower; that even Pod

conceded; as skillful in his own way as ever Pod had been. The two gentlemen would have long discussions of an evening after supper, on the finer points of a multiplex art. Pod belonged to a more moderate school: the daily sortie and modest loot—a little here, a little there—nothing to rouse suspicion. Spiller preferred a make-hay-while-the-sun-shines technique: a swift whip-round of whatever he could lay hands on and a quick getaway. This difference in approach was understandable, Arrietty thought as, listening, she helped her mother with the dishes. Pod was a house-borrower, long established in traditional routine; whereas Spiller dealt exclusively with Gypsies—here today and gone tomorrow—and must match his quickness with theirs.

Sometimes a whole week would elapse without their seeing Spiller, but he would leave them well stocked with cooked food: a haunch of this or that, or a little stew flavored with wild garlic which Homily would heat over the candle. Flour, sugar, tea, butter—even bread—they had now in plenty. Spiller, in his nonchalant way, would sooner or later provide almost anything they asked for—a piece of plum-colored velvet out of which Homily made a new skirt for Arrietty, two whole candles to augment their stub; four empty cotton reels on which they raised their table and, to Homily's joy, six mussel shells for plates.

Once he brought them a small glass medicine bottle, circular in shape. As he uncorked it, Spiller said: "Know what this is?"

Homily, wry-faced, sniffed at the amber liquid. "Some kind of hair-wash?" she asked, grimacing.

"Elder-flower wine," Spiller told her, watching her expression. "Good, that is."

Homily, about to taste, suddenly changed her mind. " 'When wine is in,' " she told Spiller— quoting from Arrietty's Diary and Proverb Book, " 'Wit is out.' Besides, I was brought up teetotal."

"He makes it in a watering can," explained Spiller, "and pours it out of the spout."

"Who does?" asked Homily.

"Mild Eye," said Spiller.

There was a short silence, tense with curiosity. "And who might Mild Eye be?" asked Homily at last. Airily pinning up her back hair, she moved slightly away from Spiller and began softly to hum below her breath.

"He that had the boot," said Spiller carelessly.

"Oh?" remarked Homily. She took up the thistle-head and began to sweep the floor—without seeming to be rude she managed to convey a gentle dismissal of the now-I-must-get-on-with-the-housework kind. "What boot?"

"This boot," said Spiller, and kicked the toe.

Homily stopped sweeping; she stared at Spiller. "But this was a gentleman's boot," she pointed out evenly.

" 'Was' is right," said Spiller.

Homily was silent a moment. "I don't understand you," she said at last.

"Afore Mild Eye pinched 'em," explained Spiller.

Homily laughed. "Mild Eye . . . Mild Eye . . . who is this Mild Eye?" she asked airily, determined not to be rattled.

"I told you," said Spiller. "The Gypsy as took up the boots."

"Boots?" repeated Homily, raising her eyebrows and stressing the plural.

"They was a pair. Mild Eye picked 'em up outside the scullery door—" Spiller jerked his head— "that big house down yonder. Went there selling clothes pegs and there they was, set out on the cobbles, pairs of 'em—all shapes and sizes, shined up nice, set out in the sunshine . . . brushes and all."

"Oh," said Homily thoughtfully—this sounded a good "borrow," "and he took the lot?"

Spiller laughed. "Not Mild Eye. Took up the pair and closed up the gap."

"I see," said Homily. After a moment she asked, "And who borrowed this one? You?"

"In a manner of speaking," said Spiller, and added, as though in part explanation, "He's got this piebald cat."

"What's the cat got to do with it?" asked Homily.

"A great Tom comes yowling round the place one night and Mild Eye ups and heaves a boot at it—this boot." Again Spiller kicked at the leather. "Good and watertight this boot was afore a weasel bit into the toe. So I gets hold of her, drags her through the hedge by the laces, heaves her into the water, jumps aboard, sails downstream to the corner, brings her aground on the mud and dries her out after, up in the long grass."

Spiller laughed. "You should have heard old Mild Eye in the morning. Knew just where he'd heaved the boot, cussin' and swearin'. Couldn't make it out." Spiller laughed again. "Never passes the way," he went on, "but he has another look."

Homily turned pale. "Another look?" she repeated nervously.

Spiller shrugged. "What's the difference? Wouldn't think to look this side of the water. Knows where he heaved the boot, Mild Eye does: that's what he can't fathom."

"Oh, my," faltered Homily unhappily.

"You've no call to worry," said Spiller. "Anything you'm wanting?"

"A bit of something woolen, I wouldn't mind," said Homily. "We was cold last night in the boot."

"Like a bit of sheep's fleece?" asked Spiller. "There's plenty down to the lane along them brambles."

"Anything," agreed Homily, "providing it's warm. And providing"—she added, suddenly struck by a horrid thought—"it ain't a sock." Her eyes widened. "I don't want no sock belonging to that Mild Eye."

Spiller dined with them that night on cold boiled minnow with sorrel salad. He had brought them a splendid wad of cleanish fleece and a strip of red rag off the end of a blanket. Pod, less teetotal than Homily, poured him out a half hazel shell of elderberry wine. But Spiller would not touch it. "I've things to do," he told them soberly, and they guessed he was off on a trip.

"Be away long?" asked Pod casually as, just to sample it, he took a sip of wine.

"A week," said Spiller, "ten days, maybe. . . ."

"Well," said Pod, "take care of yourself." He took another sip of wine. "It's nice," he told Homily, proffering the hazel shell. "You try it."

Homily shook her head and tightened her lips. "We'll miss you, Spiller," she said, batting her eyelids and ignoring Pod, "and that's a fact. . . ."

"Why have you got to go?" asked Arrietty suddenly.

Spiller, about to push his way through the screen of leaves, turned back to look at her.

Arrietty colored. I've asked him a question, she realized unhappily; now he'll disappear for weeks. But this time, Spiller seemed merely hesitant.

"Me winter clothes," he said at last.

"Oh," exclaimed Arrietty, raising her head—delighted. "New?"

Spiller nodded.

"Fur?" asked Homily.

Spiller nodded again.

"Rabbit?" asked Arrietty.

"Mole," said Spiller.

There was a sudden feeling of gaiety in the candlelit alcove: a pleasant sense of something to look forward to. All three of them smiled at Spiller and Pod raised his "glass." "To Spiller's new clothes," he said, and Spiller, suddenly embarrassed, dived quickly through the branches. But before the living curtain had stopped quivering, they saw his face again; amused and shy, it poked back at them framed in leaves. "A lady makes them," he announced self-consciously and again he disappeared.

16

"Every tide has its ebb."
Burning of the Tower of London, 1841

[Extract from Arrietty's Diary and
Proverb Book, October 30th]

Next morning early Pod, on the edge of the alcove, summoned Arrietty from the boot. "Come on out," he called, "and see this."

Arrietty, shivering, pulled on a few clothes and, wrapping the piece of red blanket around her shoulders, she crept out beside him. The sun was up and the landscape shimmered, dusted over with what, to Arrietty, looked like powdered sugar.

"This is it," said Pod, after a moment, "the first frost."

Arrietty pushed her numbed fingers under her armpits, hugging the blanket closer. "Yes," she said soberly, and they stared in silence.

After a bit, Pod cleared his throat. "There's no call to wake your mother," he said huskily. "Like as not, with this sun, it'll be clear in less than an hour." He became silent again, thinking deeply. "Thought you'd like to see it," he said at last.

"Yes," said Arrietty again and added politely, "it's pretty. . . ."

"What we better do," said Pod, "is get the breakfast quietly and leave your mother sleeping. She's all right," he went on. "She's deep in that fleece."

"I'm perished," grumbled Homily at breakfast, her hands wrapped round a half hazel shell filled with piping hot tea. There was less need, now they had Spiller, to economize on candles. "It strikes right through to the marrow. You know what?" she went on.

"No," said Pod—it was the only reply. "What?"

"Say we went down to the caravan site and had a look round? There won't be no Gypsies: when Spiller goes, it means they moved off. Might find something," she added, "and in this kind of weather, there ain't no sense in sitting around. What about it, Pod? We could wrap up warm."

Arrietty was silent, watching their faces: she had learned not to urge.

Pod hesitated. Would it be poaching, he wondered—was this Spiller's preserve? "All right," he said uncertainly, after a moment.

It was not a simple expedition. Spiller having hidden his boat, they had to ferry themselves across the water on a flat piece of bark and it was rough going when, once in the wood, they tried to follow the stream by land: both banks were thickly grown with brambles, ghastly forests of living barbed wire which tore at their hair and clothes; by the time they had scrambled through the hedge onto the stretch of grass beside the lane, they were all three disheveled and bleeding.

Arrietty looked about her at the camping site and was depressed by what she saw: this wood through which they had scrambled now shut off the last pale gleams of sun; the shadowed grass was bruised and yellow; here and there were odd bones, drifting feathers, bits of rag, and every now and again a stained newspaper flapped in the hedge.

"Oh dear," muttered Homily, glancing from side to side. "Somehow, now, I don't seem to fancy that bit o' red blanket."

"Well," said Pod after a pause, "come on. We may as well take a look round. . . ." And he led the way down the bank.

They poked about rather distastefully and Homily thought of fleas. Pod found an old iron saucepan without a bottom: he felt it might do for something but could not think for what; he walked around it speculatingly and, once or twice, he tapped it sharply with the head of his hat pin which made a dull clang. Anyway, he decided at last as he moved away, it was no good to him here and was far too heavy to move away.

Arrietty found a disused cooking stove: it was flung into the bank below the hedge—so sunk it was in the grasses and so thickly engrained with rust that it must have been there for years. "You know," she remarked to her mother, after studying it in silence, "you could live in a stove like this."

Homily stared. "In that?" she exclaimed disgustedly. The stove lay tilted, partially sunk in earth; as stoves went it was a very small one, with a barred grate and a miniature oven of the kind which are built into caravans. Beside it, they noticed a pile of whitish bones.

"Not sure she isn't right," agreed Pod, tapping the bars of the grate. "You could have a fire in here, say, and live in the oven like."

"Live!" exclaimed Homily. "Be roasted alive, you mean."

"No," explained Pod. "Needn't be a big fire. Just enough to warm the place through like. And there you'd be"—he looked at the brass latch on the door of the oven—"safe as houses. Iron, that is." He rapped the stove with his hat pin. "Nothing couldn't gnaw through that."

"Field mice could slip through them bars," said Homily.

"Maybe," said Pod, "but I wasn't thinking so much about field mice as about"—he paused uneasily—"stoats and foxes and them kind of cattle."

"Oh, Pod," exclaimed Homily, clapping her hands flat to her cheeks and making her eyes tragic, "the things you do bring up! Why do you do it?" she implored him tearfully. "Why? You know what it does to me!"

"Well, there are such things," Pod pointed out stolidly. "In this life," he went on, "you got to see what *is*, as you might say, and then face up to what you wish there wasn't."

"But foxes, Pod," protested Homily.

"Yes," agreed Pod, "but there they are; you can't deny 'em. See what I mean?"

"I see all right," said Homily, eyeing the stove more kindly, "but say you lit it, the Gypsies would see the smoke."

"And not only the Gypsies," admitted Pod, glancing aside at the lane, "anyone passing would see it. No," he sighed, as he turned to go, "this stove ain't feasible. Pity—because of the iron."

The only really comforting find of the day was a piping-hot blackened potato: Arrietty found it on the site of the Gypsies' fire. The embers were still warm, and, when stirred with a stick, a line of scarlet sparks ran snakewise through the ash. The potato steamed when they broke it open and, comforted, they ate their fill, sitting as close as they dared to the perilous warmth.

"Wish we could take a bit of this ash home," Homily remarked. "This is how Spiller cooks, I shouldn't wonder—borrows a bit of the Gypsies' fire. What do you think, Pod?"

Pod blew on his crumb of hot potato. "No," he said, taking a bite and speaking with his mouth full, "Spiller cooks regular-like whether the Gypsies are here or not. Spiller's got his own method. Wish I knew what it was."

Homily leaned forward, stirring the embers with a charred stick. "Say we kept this fire alight?" she suggested, "and brought the boot down here?"

Pod glanced about uneasily. "Too public," he said.

"Say, we put it in the hedge," went on Homily, "alongside that stove. What about that? Say we put it *in* the stove?" she added suddenly, inspired but fearful.

Pod turned slowly and looked at her. "Homily—" he began, and paused, as though stumped for words. After a moment, he laid a hand on his wife's arm and looked with some pride toward his daughter. "Your mother's a wonderful woman," he said in a moved voice. "And never you forget it, Arrietty."

Then it was "all hands to the plow": they gathered sticks like maniacs, and wet leaves to keep up the smolder. Backwards and forwards they ran, up into the hedges, along the banks, into the spinney . . . they tugged, and wrenched, and tripped and stumbled . . . and, soon, a white column of smoke spiraled up into the leaden sky.

"Oh, my," panted Homily, distressed, "folks'll see this for miles!"

"No matter," gasped Pod, as he pushed on a lichen-covered branch, "they'll think it's the Gypsies. Pile on some more of them leaves, Arrietty, we got to keep this going till morning."

A sudden puff of wind blew the smoke into Homily's eyes and the tears ran down her cheeks. "Oh, my," she exclaimed—again distressed. "This is what we'll be doing all winter, day in, day out, till we're wore to the bone and run out of fuel. It ain't no good, Pod. See what I mean?"

And she sat down suddenly on a blackened tin lid and wept in earnest. "You can't spend the rest of your life," she whimpered, "tending an open fire."

Pod and Arrietty had nothing to say: they knew suddenly that Homily was right: borrowers were too little and weak to create a full-sized blaze. The light was fading and the wind sharpening, a leaden wind which presaged snow.

"Better we start for home," said Pod, at last. "We tried anyway. Come on, now," he urged Homily, "dry your eyes; we'll think of something else. . . ."

But they didn't think of anything else. And the weather became colder. There was no sign of Spiller and, after ten days, they ran out of meat and started (their sole source of warmth) on the last bit of candle.

"I don't know," Homily would moan unhappily, as at night they crept under the fleece, "what we're going to do I'm sure. We won't see Spiller again, that's one thing certain. Daresay he's met with an accident."

Then came the snow. Homily, tucked up in the boot, would not get up to see it. To her, it meant the end. "I'll die here," she announced, "tucked up comfortable. You and Father," she told Arrietty, "can die where you like."

It was no good Arrietty assuring her that the field looked very pretty, that the cold seemed less severe, and that she had made a sled of the blackened tin lid which Pod had retrieved from the ashes: she had made her grave and was determined to lie in it.

In spite of this and rather heartlessly, Arrietty

still enjoyed her toboggan runs down the bank with a wide sweep into the ditch at the bottom. And Pod, brave soul, still went out to forage—though there was little left to eat in the hedgerows and for this little, a few remaining berries, they had to compete with the birds. Though appreciably thinner, none of them felt ill and Arrietty's snow-tanned cheeks glowed with a healthy color.

But five days later, it was a different story: intense cold and a second fall of snow—snow which piled up in air-filled drifts, too light and feathery to support a matchstick, let alone a borrower. They became housebound and, for most of the time, joined Homily in the boot. The fleece was warm but, lying there in semidarkness, the time passed slowly and the days were very boring. Homily would revive occasionally and tell them stories of her childhood: she could be as long-winded as she liked with this audience which could not get away.

They came to an end of the food. "There's nothing left," announced Pod, one evening, "but one lump of sugar and a quarter inch of candle."

"I couldn't never eat that," complained Homily, "not paraffin wax."

"No one's asking you to," said Pod. "And we've still that drop of elderberry wine."

Homily sat up in bed. "Ah!" she said, "put the

sugar in the wine and heat it up over the quarter inch of candle."

"But, Homily," protested Pod, surprised. "I thought you was teetotal."

"Grog's different," explained Homily. "Call me when it's ready," and she lay down again, piously closing her eyes.

"She will have her way," muttered Pod, aside to Arrietty. He eyed the bottle dubiously. "There's more there than I thought there was. I hope she'll be all right. . . ."

It was quite a party, so long it had been since they had lit the candle, and it was pleasant to gather round it and feel its warmth.

When at last, warmed and befuddled, they snuggled down in the fleece, a curious contentment filled Arrietty—a calmness akin to hope. Pod, she noticed, drowsed with wine, had forgotten to lace up the boot . . . well, perhaps it didn't matter—if it was their last night on earth.

17

"What Heaven will, no frost can kill."
Great Earthquake at Lisbon, 50,000 killed, 1755

[Extract from Arrietty's Diary and
Proverb Book, November 1st]

It was not their last night on earth: it seldom is, somehow; it was, however, their last night *in* earth.

Arrietty was the first to wake. She woke tired, as though she had slept badly, but it was only later, as she told Tom, that she remembered her dream of the earthquake. She not only woke tired but she woke cramped, and in a most uncomfortable position. There seemed more light than was usual and then she remembered the unlaced opening. But why, she wondered, as she roused a little, did the daylight seem to come in from above, as from a half-concealed skylight? And suddenly she understood— the boot, which lay always on its side, for some extraordinary reason was standing upright. Her first thought—and it made her heart beat faster—was that her dream of an earthquake had been fact. She glanced at Pod and Homily: from what she could see of them, so enmeshed they were in fleece, they appeared to be sleeping soundly but not, she thought, quite in the same positions as when they had gone to bed. Something had happened—she was sure of it—unless she still was dreaming.

Stealthily Arrietty sat up; although the boot was open, the air felt surprisingly warm—almost stuffy; it smelt of woodsmoke and onions and of something else—a smell she could not define—could it be the scent of a human being?

Arrietty crept along the sole of the boot until she stood under the opening. Staring up she saw, instead of the sandy roof of the annex, a curious network of wire springs and some kind of striped ceiling. They must be under some bed, she realized—she had seen this view of beds back home—but what bed? And where?

Trembling a little but too curious not to be brave, she put her foot as high as she could into an eyelet hole and pulled herself erect on a loop of shoelace; another step up, a harder pull—and she found she could see out: the first thing she saw, standing close beside her—so close that she could see into it— was a second boot exactly like their own.

That was about all she could see from her present position: the bed was low, stretching up she could almost touch the springs with her hands. But she could hear things—the liquid purr of a simmering kettle, the crack of a fire, and a deeper more rhythmic sound—the sound of a human snore.

Arrietty hesitated: she was in half a mind to wake her parents, but, on second thoughts, she decided against it. First to find out a bit more. She unloosed a couple of lace-holes and eased out through the gap and, via the boot's instep, she walked out to the toe. Now she could really see.

As she had guessed, they were in a caravan. The boots stood under a collapsible bed which ran along one side of its length; and facing her on the opposite side, parallel to this bed she saw a miniature coal range very like the one in the hedge, and a light-grained overmantel. The shelves of the overmantel, she saw, were set with pieces of looking glass and adorned with painted vases, old coronation mugs and trails of paper flowers. Below and on each side were set-in drawers and cupboards. A kettle simmered gently on the flat of the stove and a fire glowed redly through the bars.

At right angles, across the rear end of the caravan, she saw a second bunk, built in more permanently above a locker, and the locker she noted, thinking of cover, was not set in flush with the floor: there was space below into which, if crouching, a borrower might creep. In the bunk above the locker, she saw a heaving mountain of patchwork which she knew must contain, by the sound of the snoring, a human being asleep. Beside the head of the bunk stood a watering can, a tin mug balanced on the spout. Elder-flower wine, she thought—that last night had been their undoing.

To her left, also at right angles, was the door of the caravan, the top half open to the winter sunshine; it faced, she knew, toward the shafts. A crack of sunlight ran down the latch side of this door—a crack through which, if she dared approach it, she might perhaps see out.

She hesitated. It was only a step to the crack— a yard and a half at most: the human mountain was still heaving, filling the air with sound. Lightly, Arrietty slid from the toe of the boot to the worn piece of carpet and, soundless in her stockinged feet, she tiptoed to the door. For a moment, the sunlight striking almost brightly through the crack seemed to blind her, then she made out a stretch of dirty grass, sodden with melting snow, a fire smoking sulkily between two stones, and beyond that, some way distant below the hedge, she saw a familiar object—the remains of a disused stove. Her spirits rose: so they were still at the same old caravan site—they had not, as she had feared at first, been traveling in the night.

As, her nose in the crack, she stood there staring, a sudden silence behind her caused her to turn; and, having turned, she froze: the human being was sitting up in bed. He was a huge man, fully dressed, dark-skinned, and with a mass of curling hair; his eyes were screwed up, his fists stretched and his mouth wide open in a long-drawn, groaning yawn.

Panic-stricken, she thought about cover. She glanced at the bed to her right—the bed under which she had awakened. Three strides would do it: but better to be still, that's what Pod would say: the shadowed part of the door against which she stood would seem still darker because of that opened half above, filled so brightly with winter sunshine. All Arrietty did was to move aside from the crack of light against whose brightness she might be outlined.

The human being stopped yawning and swung his legs down from the bunk and sat there a moment, pensively, admiring his stockinged feet. One of his eyes, Arrietty noticed, was dark and twinkling, the other paler, hazel-yellow, with a strangely drooping lid. This must be Mild Eye—this great, fat, terrifying man, who sat so quietly smiling at his feet.

As Arrietty watched, the strange eyes lifted a little and the smile broadened: Mild Eye, Arrietty saw, was looking at the boots.

She caught her breath as she saw him lean forward and (a stretch of the long arm was enough) snatch them up from below the other bed. He examined them lovingly, holding them together as a pair, and then, as though struck by some discrepancy in the weight, he set one down on the floor. He shook the other gently, turning its opening toward his palm and, as nothing fell out, he put his hand inside.

The shout he gave, Arrietty thought afterwards, must have been heard for miles. He dropped the boot, which fell on its side and Arrietty, in an anguish of terror, saw Homily and Pod run out and disappear between his legs (but not, she realized, before he had glimpsed them) into the shallow space between his bunk and the floor.

There was a horrified pause.

Arrietty was scared enough, but Mild Eye seemed even more so: his two strange eyes bulged in a face which had turned the color of putty. Two tiny words hung in the silence, a thread-thin echo, incredible to Mild Eye: someone . . . something . . . somewhere . . . on a note of anguish, had stammered out, "Oh dear!"

And that was controlled enough, Arrietty thought, for what Homily must be feeling: to be woken from a deep sleep and shaken out of the boot; to have seen those two strange eyes staring down at her; to

have heard that thunderous shout. The space between the locker and the floor, Arrietty calculated, could not be more than a couple of inches; it would be impossible to stand up in there and, although safe enough for the moment, there they would have to stay: there seemed no possible way out.

For herself—glued motionless against the shadows—she was less afraid: true enough she stood face to face with Mild Eye; but he would not see her, of this she felt quite sure, providing she did not move: he seemed too shaken by those half-glimpsed creatures which so inexplicably had appeared between his feet.

Stupefied, he stared for a moment longer; then awkwardly he got down on all fours and peered under the locker; as though disappointed, he got up again, found a box of matches, struck a light and once again explored the shadows as far as the light would carry. Arrietty took advantage of his turned back to take her three strides and slip back under the bed. There was a cardboard box under here, which she could use as cover, some ends of rope, a bundle of rabbit snares and a slimy saucer which once had contained milk.

She made her way between these objects until she reached the far end—the junction of the bed with the locker below the bunk. Peering out through the tangle of rabbit snares, she saw that Mild Eye—despairing of matchlight—had armed himself with a hefty knob-kerrystick which he was now running back and forth in a businesslike manner along the space between the bunk and the floor. Arrietty, her hands pressed tight against her heart, once thought she heard a strangled squeak and a muttered "Oh, my gracious . . . !"

At that moment, the door of the caravan opened, there was a draft of cold air, and a wild-eyed woman looked in. Wrapped in a heavy shawl against the cold, she was carrying a basket of clothes pegs. Arrietty, crouching among the rabbit snares, saw the wild eyes open still more wildly and a flood of questions in some foreign tongue was aimed at Mild Eye's behind. Arrietty saw the woman's breath smoke in the clear sunshine and could hear her earrings jangle.

Mild Eye, a little shamefaced, rose to his feet; he looked very big to Arrietty and, though she could no longer see his face, his hanging hands looked helpless. He replied to the woman in the same language: he said quite a lot; sometimes his voice rose on a curious squeak of dismayed excitement.

He picked up the boot, showed it to the woman, said a lot about it and—somewhat nervously, Arrietty noticed—he put his hand inside; he pulled out the wad of fleece, the unraveled sock, and—with some surprise because it had once been his—the strip of colored blanket. As he showed these to the woman, who continued to jeer, his voice became almost tearful. The woman laughed then—a thin, high peal of raucous laughter. Completely heartless, Arrietty thought, completely unkind. She wanted almost for Mild Eye's sake to run out and show this doubting creature that there were such things as borrowers ("It's so awful and sad," she once admitted to Tom Goodenough, "to belong to a race that no sane person believes in"). But tempting as this thought was, she thought better of it and instead she edged herself out from the end of the bed into the darker space below the bunk.

And only just in time: there was a faint thud on the carpet, and there, not a foot from where she had stood, she saw the four paws of a cat—three black and one white; she saw him stretch, roll over and rub his whiskered face on the sun-warmed carpet: he was black, she saw, with a white belly and a white patch over one eye. He or she? Arrietty did not know: a fine beast, anyway, sleek and heavy as cats are who hunt for themselves out-of-doors.

Sidling crabwise into the shadows, her eyes on the basking cat, she felt her hand taken suddenly, held and squeezed tight. "Oh, thank goodness . . ."

Homily breathed in her ear, "thank heavens you're safe."

Arrietty put a finger to her lips. "Hush," she whispered barely above her breath, staring toward the cat.

"It can't get under here," whispered Homily. Her face, Arrietty saw, looked pallid in the half-light, gray and streaked with dust. "We're in a caravan," she went on, determined to tell the news.

"I know," said Arrietty, and pleaded, "Mother, we'd better be quiet."

Homily was silent a moment, then she said, "He caught your father's back with that stick. The soft part," she added reassuringly.

"Hush," whispered Arrietty again. She could not see much from where she was but Mild Eye, she gathered, was struggling into a coat; after a moment, he stooped and his hand came near when he felt under the settee for the bundle of rabbit snares; the woman was still out-of-doors busy about the fire.

After a while, her eyes growing used to the dimness, Arrietty saw her father sitting some way back, leaning against the wall. She crawled across to him, and Homily followed.

"Well, here we are," said Pod, barely moving his lips, "and not dead yet," he added, with a glance at Homily.

18

"Hidden troubles disquiet most."
Gun Powder Plot, 1605

[Extract from Arrietty's Diary and
Proverb Book, November 5th]

They crouched there listening; holding their breaths as Mild Eye unlatched the door, relatched it, and clumped off down the steps.

There was a pause.

"We're alone now," remarked Homily at last in her ordinary speaking voice, "I mean, we could get out, I shouldn't wonder, if it weren't for that cat."

"Hush—" whispered Pod: he had heard the woman shoot some mocking question at Mild Eye and, at Mild Eye's mumbled reply, the woman had laughed her laugh. Arrietty, too, was listening.

"*He* knows we're here," she whispered, "but *she* won't believe him . . ."

"And that cat'll know we're here, too, soon enough," replied Pod.

Arrietty shivered: the cat, she realized, must have been asleep on the bed, while she, Arrietty, had been standing alone by the door.

Pod was silent awhile, thinking deeply. "Yes," he said at last, "it's a rum go: he must have come round at dusk last night, seeing after his snares . . . and there he finds his lost boot in our hollow."

"We should have pulled down the screen," whispered Arrietty.

"We should that," agreed Pod.

"We didn't even lace up the boot," went on Arrietty.

"Yes," said Pod and sighed. "A bottle at night and you're out like light. That how it goes?" he asked.

"More or less," agreed Arrietty in a whisper.

They sat waist-high in dusty trails of fluff. "Disgusting," remarked Homily, suppressing a sneeze. "If I'd built this caravan," she grumbled, "I'd have set the bunk in flush with the floor."

"Then thank goodness you didn't build it," remarked Pod, as a whiskered shadow appeared between them and the light: the cat had seen them at last.

"Don't panic," he went on calmly as Homily gave a gasp. "This bunk's too low; we're all right here."

"Oh, my goodness," whispered Homily, as she saw a luminous eye. Pod squeezed her hand to silence her.

The cat, having sniffed its way along the length of the opening, lay down suddenly on its side and ogled them through the gap: quite friendly, it looked, and a little coy: as though coaxing them out to play.

"They don't *know*," whispered Homily then, referring to cats in general.

"You keep still," whispered Pod.

For a long time nothing much happened: the shaft of sunshine moved slowly across the worn carpet and the cat, motionless, seemed to doze.

"Well," whispered Homily, after a while, "in a way, it's kind of nice to be indoors."

Once the woman came in and fumbled in the dresser for a wooden spoon and took away the kettle; they heard her swearing as she tended the outdoor fire and once a gust of acrid smoke blew in through the doorway, making Arrietty cough. The cat woke up at that and cocked an eye at them.

Toward midday, they smelt a savory smell—the gamy smell of stew: it would drift toward them as the wind veered and then, tormentingly, would drift away.

Arrietty felt her mouth water.

"*Oh*, I'm hungry . . ." she sighed.

"I'm thirsty," said Homily.

"I'm both," said Pod. "Now be quiet, the two

of you," he told them. "Shut your eyes and think of something else."

"Whenever I shut my eyes," protested Homily, "I see a nice hot thimbleful of tea, or I think of that teapot we had back home: that oak-apple teapot, with a quill spout."

"Well, think of it," said Pod, "no harm in that, if it does you good——"

The man came back at last. He unlatched the door and threw a couple of snared rabbits down on the carpet. He and the woman ate their meal on the steps of the caravan, using the floor as a table.

At this point the smell of food became unbearable: it drew the three borrowers out of the shadows to the very edge of their shelter: the tin plates, filled with savory stew, were at eye level; they had a splendid view of the floury potatoes, and the richly running gravy. "Oh, my . . ." muttered Homily unhappily, "pheasant—and what a way to eat it!"

Once Mild Eye threw a morsel on the carpet. Enviously they watched the cat pounce and leisurely fall to, crunching up the bones like the hunter it was. "Oh, my . . ." muttered Homily again, "those teeth!"

At length Mild Eye pushed aside his plate. The cat stared with interest at the pile of chewed bones to which here and there clung slivers of tender meat. Homily stared, too: the plate was almost in range. "Dare you, Pod?" she whispered.

"No," said Pod—so loudly and firmly that the cat turned round and looked at him; gaze met gaze with curious mutual defiance; the cat's tail began slowly to swish from side to side.

"Come on," gasped Pod, as the cat crouched, and all three dodged back into the shadows in the split half-second before the pounce.

Mild Eye turned quickly. Staring, he called to the woman, pointing toward the bunk, and both man and woman stooped their heads to floor level, gazing across the carpet . . . and gazing, it seemed to Arrietty, crouched with her parents against the back wall of the caravan, right into their faces. It seemed impossible that they could not be seen: but—"It's all right," Pod told them, speaking with still lips in the lightest of whispers, "don't panic—just you keep still."

There was silence: even the woman now seemed uneasy—the cat, padding and peering, back and forth along the length of the locker, had aroused her curiosity. "Don't you move," breathed Pod again.

A sudden shadow fell across the patch of sunlight on the carpet: a third figure, Arrietty noted with surprise, loomed up behind the crouching Gyp-

sies in the doorway: someone less tall than Mild
Eye. Arrietty, rigid between her parents, saw three
buttons of a stained corduroy waistcoat and, as its
wearer stooped, she saw a young face, and a tow-
colored head of hair. "What's up?" asked a voice
which had a crack in it.

Arrietty saw Mild Eye's expression change: it
became all at once sulky and suspicious. He turned
slowly and faced the speaker, but before he did so,
he slid his right hand inconspicuously across the
floor of the caravan, pushing the two dead rabbits
out of sight.

"What's up, Mild Eye?" asked the boy again.
"Looks like you'm seeing ghosties."

Mild Eye shrugged his great shoulders. "Maybe
I am," he said.

The boy stooped again, staring along the floor
and Arrietty could see that, under one arm, he carried a gun. "Wouldn't be a ferret by any chance?"
he asked slyly.

The woman laughed then. "A ferret!" she exclaimed and laughed again. "You're the one for
ferrets. . . ." Pulling her shawl more tightly about
her, she moved away toward the fire. "You think
the cat act *kind* like that for a ferret?"

The boy stared curiously past the cat across the
floor, screwing his eyelids to see beyond the pacing

cat and into the shadows. "The cat b'ain't acting so kind," he remarked thoughtfully.

"A couple of midgets he's got in there," the woman told him. "Dressed up to kill—or so he says," and she went off again into screams of jeering laughter.

The boy did not laugh; his expression did not change: calmly he stared at the crack below the bunk. "Dressed up to kill . . ." he repeated and, after a moment, he added, "Only two?"

"How many do you want?" asked the woman, "half a dozen? A couple's enough, ain't it?"

"What do you reckon to do with them?" asked the boy.

"Do with them?" repeated the woman, staring stupidly.

"I mean, when you catch them?"

The woman gave him a curious look, as though doubting his reason. "But there ain't nothing there," she told him.

"But you just said—"

The woman laughed, half angry, half bewil-

dered. "Mild Eye sees 'em—not me. Or so he makes out! There ain't nothing there, I tell you . . ."

"I see 'em all right," said Mild Eye; he stretched his fist finger and thumb, "this high, I'd say—a bit of a woman, it looked like, and a bit of a man."

"Mind if I look?" asked the boy, his foot on the steps. He laid down his gun and Arrietty, watching, saw him put his hand in his pocket; there was a stealthiness about his movement which drove the blood from her heart. "Oh," she gasped and grabbed her father's sleeve.

"What is it?" breathed Pod, leaning toward her.

"His pocket—" stammered Arrietty, "something alive in his pocket!"

"A ferret," cried Homily, forgetting to whisper. "We're finished."

"Hush—" implored Pod: the boy had heard something; he had seated himself on the top step and was now leaning forward gazing toward them across the strip of faded carpet. At Homily's exclamation, Pod had seen his eyes widen, his face become alert.

"What's the good of whispering?" complained Homily, lowering her voice all the same. "We're for it now. Wouldn't matter if we sang . . ."

"Hush—" said Pod again.

"How would you think to get 'em out?" the boy

was asking, his eyes on the gap; his right hand, Arrietty saw, still feeling in his pocket.

"Easy," explained Mild Eye, "empty the locker and take up them boards underneath."

"You see?" whispered Homily, almost in triumph. "It doesn't matter what we do now!"

Pod gave up. "Then sing," he suggested wearily.

"Nailed down, them boards are, aren't they?" asked the boy.

"No," said Mild Eye. "I've had 'em out after rats; they comes out in a piece."

The boy, his head lowered, was staring into the gap: Arrietty from where she crouched was looking straight into his eyes: they were thoughtful eyes, bland and blue.

"Say you catch them," the boy went on, "what then?"

"What then?" repeated Mild Eye, puzzled.

"What do you want to do with 'em?"

"Do with 'em? Cage 'em up. What else?"

"Cage 'em up in what?"

"In that." Mild Eye touched the bird cage, which swung slightly. "What else?"

("And feed us on groundsel, I shouldn't wonder," muttered Homily below her breath.)

"You want to keep 'em?" asked the boy, his eyes on the shadowed gap.

"Keep 'em, naow! Sell 'em!" exclaimed Mild Eye. "Fetch a pretty penny, that lot would—cage and all complete."

("Oh, my goodness," whimpered Homily.

"Quiet," breathed Pod, "better the cage than the ferret."

"No," thought Arrietty, "better the ferret.")

"What would you feed 'em on?" the boy was asking; he seemed to be playing for time.

Mild Eye laughed indulgently. "Anything. Bits o' leftovers . . ."

("You hear that?" whispered Homily, very angry.

"Well, today it was pheasant," Pod reminded her; but he was glad she was angry: anger made her brave.)

Mild Eye had climbed right in, now—blotting out the sunshine. "Move over," he said to the boy, "we got to get at the locker."

The boy shifted, a token shift. "What about the cat?" he said.

"That's right," agreed Mild Eye, "better have the cat out. Come on, Tiger—"

But the cat, it seemed, was as stubborn as the boy and shared his interest in borrowers; evading Mild Eye's hand, it sprang away to the bed and (Arrietty gathered from a slight thud immediately above their heads) from the end of the bed to the locker. Mild Eye came after it: they could see his great feet close against the gap—their own dear boot was there just beside them, with the patch which Pod had sewn! It seemed incredible to see it worn, and by such a hostile foot.

"Better cart it out to the missus," suggested the boy, as Mild Eye grabbed the cat, "if it b'ain't held onto it'll only jump back in."

("Don't you dare—" moaned Homily, just below her breath.

Pod looked amazed. "Who are you talking to?" he asked in a whisper.

"Him—Mild Eye: the minute he leaves this caravan that boy'll be after us with the ferret."

"Now, see here—" began Pod.

"You mark my words," went on Homily in a panic-stricken whisper. "I know who he is, now. It's all come back to me: young Tom Goodenough. I heard speak of that one many a time back home under the kitchen. And I wouldn't be surprised if it wasn't him we saw at the window—that day we made off, remember? Proper devil, he's reckoned to be with that ferret—"

"Quiet, Homily!" implored Pod.

"Why? For heavens' sakes—they know we're here: quiet or noisy—what's the difference?")

2 0 5

Mild Eye swore suddenly as though the cat had scratched him. "Cart him right out," said the boy again, "and see she holds him."

"Don't fret," said Mild Eye. "We can shut the door."

"That b'ain't no good," said the boy. "We can't shut the top half; we got to have light."

On the threshold Mild Eye hesitated. "Don't you touch nothin'," he said, and stood there a moment, waiting before he clumped off down the steps. On the bottom rung he seemed to slip: the borrowers could hear him swearing. "This blamed boot," they heard him say and something about the heel.

"You all right?" called out the boy carelessly. The answer was an oath.

"Block your ears," whispered Homily to Arrietty. "Oh, my goodness me, did you hear what he said?"

"Yes," began Arrietty obligingly, "he said—"

"Oh, you wicked, heathen girl," cried Homily angrily. "Shame on yourself for listening!"

"Quiet, Homily," begged Pod again.

"But you know what happened, Pod?" whispered Homily excitedly. "The heel came off the boot! What did I tell you, up in the ditch, when you would take out them nails?" For one brief moment she forgot her fears and gave a tiny giggle.

"Look," breathed Arrietty suddenly and reached for her mother's hand. They looked.

The boy, leaning toward them on one elbow, his steady gaze fixed on the slit of darkness between the locker and floor, was feeling stealthily in the right hand pocket of his coat—it was the deep, pouched pocket common to gamekeepers.

"Oh, my . . ." muttered Homily as Pod took her hand.

"Shut your eyes," said Pod. "No use running and you won't know nothing: a ferret strikes quick."

There was a pause, tense and solemn, while three small hearts beat quickly. Homily broke it.

"I've tried to be a good wife to you, Pod," she announced tearfully, one eye screwed obediently shut, the other cautiously open.

"You've been first-rate," said Pod, his eyes on the boy: against the light, it was hard to see, but something moved in his hand: a creature he had taken from his pocket.

"A bit sharp sometimes," went on Homily.

"It doesn't matter now," said Pod.

"I'm sorry, Pod," said Homily.

"I forgive you," said Pod absently; a deeper shadow now had fallen across the carpet: Mild Eye had come back up the steps. Pod saw the woman had sneaked up behind him, clasping the cat in her shawl.

The boy did not start or turn. "Make for my pocket . . ." he said steadily, his eyes on the gap.

"What's that?" asked Mild Eye, surprised.

"Make for my pocket," repeated the boy. "Do you hear what I say?" And suddenly he loosed on the carpet the thing he had held in his hand.

"Oh, my goodness—" cried Homily, clutching on to Pod.

"Whatever is it?" she went on, after a moment, both eyes suddenly open: some kind of living creature it was, but certainly not a ferret . . . too slow . . . too angular . . . too upright . . . too—

Arrietty let out a glad cry. "It's Spiller!"

"What?" exclaimed Homily, almost crossly—tricked she felt, when she thought of those splendid "last words."

"It's Spiller," Arrietty sang out again. "Spiller . . . Spiller . . . Spiller!"

"Looking quite ridiculous," remarked Homily: and indeed he did look rather odd and sausage-like, stuffed out in his stiff new clothes. He would render them down gradually to a wearable suppleness.

"What are you waiting for?" asked Spiller. "You heard what he said. Come on now. Get moving, can't you?"

"That boy?" exclaimed Homily. "Was he speaking to us?"

"Who else?" snapped Spiller. "He don't want Mild Eye in his pocket. Come on—"

"His pocket!" exclaimed Homily in a frantic whisper; she turned to Pod. "Now let's get this right: young Tom Goodenough wants me"—she touched her own chest—"to run out there, right in the open, get meself over his trouser-leg, across his middle, up to his hip, and potter down all meek and mild into his pocket?"

"Not you only," explained Pod; "all of us."

"He's crazy," announced Homily firmly, tightening her lips.

"Now, see here, Homily," began Pod.

"I'd sooner perish," Homily asserted.

"That's just what you will do," said Pod.

"Remember that peg-bag?" she reminded him. "I couldn't face it, Pod. And where's he going to take us? Tell me that?"

"How should I know?" exclaimed Pod. "Now, come on, Homily, you do what he says, there's me brave old girl . . . Take her by the wrist, Spiller, she's got to come . . . Ready, Arrietty? Now for it—" and suddenly there they were, the whole group of them—out in the open.

19

"Fortune favors the brave."
Sherman's March to the Coast began, 1864

[Extract from Arrietty's Diary and
Proverb Book, November 13th]

The woman screeched when she saw them: she dropped the cat, and ran for her life making hell-for-leather toward the main road. Mild Eye, too, was taken aback: he sat down on the bed with his feet in the air as though a contaminated flood were swirling across the carpet: the cat, unnerved by the general uproar, made a frantic leap for the overmantel, bringing down two mugs, a framed photograph and a spray of paper rosebuds.

Pod and Arrietty made their own slithering way across the folds of trouser-leg to the rising slope of hip; but poor Spiller, pulling and pushing a protesting Homily, was picked up and dropped in. For one awful moment, attached by the wrist to Spiller, Homily dangled in air, before the boy's quick fingers gathered her up and tidied her neatly away. Only just in time—for Mild Eye, recovering, had made a sudden grab, missing her by inches ("Torn us apart, he would have," she said later, "like a couple of bananas!"): deep in the pocket, she heard his angry shout of "Four of 'em you got there. Come on: fair's fair—hand over them first two!"

They did not know what happened next: all was darkness and jumble. Some sort of struggle was going on—there was the sound of heavy breathing, muttered swear words and the pocket swayed and bounced. Then, by the bumping, they knew the boy was running and Mild Eye, shouting behind him, was cursing his heelless boot. They heard these shouts grow fainter; and the crackle of breaking branches as the boy crashed through a hedge.

There was no conversation in the pocket: all four of them felt too dazed. At last Pod, wedged upside down in a corner, freed his mouth from fluff. "You all right, Homily?" he gasped. Homily, tightly interwoven with Spiller and Arrietty, could not quite tell. Pod heard a slight squeak. "Me leg's gone numb," said Homily unhappily.

"Not broken, is it?" asked Pod anxiously.

"Can't feel nothing in it," said Homily.

"Can you move it?" asked Pod.

There was a sharp exclamation from Spiller as Homily said, "No."

"If it's the leg you're pinching," remarked Spiller, "stands to reason you can't move it."

"How do you know?" asked Homily.

"Because it's mine," he said.

The boy's steps became slower: he seemed to be going uphill; after a while he sat down. The great hand came down amongst them. Homily began to whimper but the fingers slid past her: they were feeling for Spiller. The coat was pulled round and the pocket flap held open, so the boy could peer at them. "You all right, Spiller?" he asked.

Spiller grunted.

"Which is Homily?" asked the boy.

"The noisy one," said Spiller. "I told you."

"You all right, Homily?" asked the boy.

Homily, terrified, was silent.

The great fingers came down again, sliding their way into the pocket.

Spiller, standing now with legs apart and back supported against the upright seam called out tersely, "Leave 'em be."

The fingers stopped moving. "I wanted to see if they were all right," said the boy.

"They're all right," said Spiller.

"I'd like to have 'em out," the boy went on. "I'd like to have a look at 'em." He peered downwards at the open pocket. "You're not dead, are you?" he inquired anxiously. "You b'ain't none of you dead?"

"How could we say, if we was?" muttered Homily irritably.

"You leave 'em be," said Spiller again. "It's warm in here: you don't want to bring 'em out sudden into the cold. You'll see 'em often enough," he consoled the boy, "once we get indoors."

The fingers withdrew and they were in the dark again: there was a rocking and the boy stood up. Pod, Homily, and Arrietty slid the length of the bottom seam of the pocket, fetching up against the opposite corner: it was full of dried bread crumbs, jagged and hard as concrete. "Ouch!" cried Homily unhappily. Spiller, Arrietty noticed, though he swayed on his feet, managed to keep upright: Spiller, she guessed, had traveled by pocket before: the boy was walking again now, and the coat swayed with a more predictable rhythm. "After a while," Arrietty thought, "I'll have a go at standing myself."

Pod experimentally broke off a jagged piece of bread crumb which, after patient sucking, slowly began to dissolve. "I'll try a bit of that," said Homily, holding out her hand; she had revived a little and was feeling peckish.

"Where's he taking us?" she asked Spiller after a while.

"Round the wood and over the hill."

"Where he lives with his grandpa?"

"That's right," admitted Spiller.

"I ain't ever heard tell much about gamekeepers," said Homily, "nor what they'd be apt to do with—a borrower, say. Nor what sort of boy this is neither. I mean," she went on in a worried voice, "my mother-in-law had an uncle once who was kept in a tin box with four holes in the lid and fed twice a day by an eyedropper . . ."

"He ain't that sort of boy," said Spiller.

"Whatever's an eyedropper?" asked Pod: he took it to be some strange sort of craft or profession.

"Then there was Lupy's cousin, Oggin, you remember," went on Homily. "They made a regular kind of world for him in the bottom of an old tin bath in the outhouse, grass, pond and all. And they gave him a cart to ride in and a lizard for company. But the sides of the bath were good and slippery: they knew he couldn't get out . . ."

"Lupy?" repeated Spiller wonderingly. "Wouldn't be two called that?"

"This one married my brother Hendreary," said Homily. "Why," she exclaimed with sudden excitement, "you don't say you know her!"

The pocket had stopped swaying: they heard some metallic sound and the sliding squeak of a latch.

"I know her all right," whispered Spiller. "She makes my winter clothes."

"Quiet," urged Pod, "we've arrived." He had heard the sound of an opening door and could smell an indoor smell.

"You know LUPY?" Homily persisted, unaware that even the pocket had become darker. "But what are they doing? And where are they living—she and Hendreary? We thought they was eaten by foxes, children and all . . ."

"Quiet, Homily," implored Pod. Strange movements seemed to be going on, doors were opening and shutting; so stealthily the boy was walking the pocket now hung still.

"Tell us, Spiller, quick," went on Homily; but she dropped her voice to an obedient whisper. "You must know! Where are they living now?"

Spiller hesitated—in the semidarkness he seemed to smile.

"They're living here," he said.

The boy now seemed to be kneeling.

As the fingers came down again feeling amongst them, Homily let out a cry. "It's all right," whispered Pod as she burrowed back among the crumbs. "Keep your head—we got to come out sometime."

Spiller went first; he sailed away from them—nonchalantly astride a finger, without even bothering to glance back. Then it was Arrietty's turn. "Oh, my goodness me . . ." muttered Homily, "where ever will they put her?"

Pod's turn next; but Homily went with him. She scrambled aboard at the last moment by creeping under the thumb. There was hardly time to feel sick (it was the swoosh through the empty air which Homily always dreaded) so deftly and gently they found themselves set down.

A gleam of firelight struck the tiny group as they stood beside the hearth, against a high, wooden wall: it was, they discovered later, the side of the log-box. They stood together—close and scared, controlling their longing to run. Spiller, they noticed, had disappeared.

The boy, on one knee, towered above them—a terrifying mountain of flesh. The firelight flickered on his down-turned face: they could feel the draught of his breathing.

"It's all right," he assured them, "you'll be all right now." He was staring with great interest, as a collector would stare at a newfound specimen. His hand hovered above them as though he longed to touch them, to pick one of them up, to examine each more closely.

Nervously Pod cleared his throat. "Where's Spiller?" he asked.

"He'll be back," said the boy. After a moment, he added, "I got six altogether in there."

"Six what?" asked Homily nervously.

"Six borrowers," said the boy, "I reckon I got the best collection of borrowers in two counties. And—" he added, "me granddad ain't seen one, though his eyes is sharp enough. Yet he ain't ever seen a borrower."

Pod cleared his throat again. "He ain't supposed to," he said.

"Some I got in there—" the boy jerked his head toward the log-box, "I never sees neither. Scared. Some folks say you can't never tame 'em. You can give 'em the earth, 'tis said, but they'll never come out and be civil."

"I would," said Arrietty.

"Now you behave yourself," snapped Homily, alarmed.

"Spiller would, too," said Arrietty.

"Spiller's different," replied Homily with a nervous glance toward the boy—Spiller, she felt, was the boy's curator: the go-between of this rare collection. "Gets so much a head, I wouldn't wonder?"

"Here he is," said Arrietty, looking toward the corner of the log-box.

Noiselessly, he had come upon them.

"She won't come out," said Spiller to the boy.

"Oh," exclaimed Homily, "does he mean Lupy?"

No one answered: Spiller stood silent, looking up at the boy. The boy frowned thoughtfully; he seemed disappointed. He looked them over once more, examining each of them from head to foot as though loath to see them go; he sighed a little. "Then, take 'em in," he said.

20

"Long looked for comes at last."
Vasco da Gama rounded
Cape of Good Hope, 1497

[Extract from Arrietty's Diary and
Proverb Book, November 20th]

They filed in through the gothic-shaped hole in the wainscot, a little nervous, a little shy. It was shadowy inside, like a cave; disappointingly it felt uninhabited and smelled of dust and mice. "Oh, dear," muttered Homily incredulously, "is this how they live . . . ?" She stopped suddenly and picked up some object from the floor. "My goodness," she whispered aside excitedly to Pod. "Do you know what this is?" and she brandished something whiteish under his nose.

"Yes," said Pod, "it's a bit of quill pipe cleaner. Put it down, Homily, and come on, do. Spiller's waiting."

"It's the spout of our old oak-apple teapot," persisted Homily, "that's what it is. I'd know it anywhere and it's no good telling me any different. So they *are* here . . ." she mused wonderingly as she followed Pod into the shadows to where Spiller with Arrietty stood waiting.

"We go up here," said Spiller, and Homily saw that he stood with his hand on a ladder. Glancing up to where the rungs soared away above them into dimness, she gave a slight shudder: the ladder was made of matchsticks, neatly glued and spliced to two lengths of split cane, such as florists use to support potted plants.

"I'll go first," said Pod. "We better take it one at a time."

Homily watched fearfully until she heard his voice from above.

"It's all right," he whispered from some invisible eyrie. "Come on up."

Homily followed, her knees trembling, and emerged at last on to the dim-lit platform beside Pod: an aerial landing stage, that was what it seemed like—which creaked a little when she stepped on it and almost seemed to sway. Below lay hollow darkness; ahead an open door. "Oh, my goodness," she muttered. "I do hope it's safe . . . Don't look down," she advised Arrietty who came up next.

But Arrietty had no temptation to look down: her eyes were on the lighted doorway and the moving shadows within; she heard the faint sound of voices and a sudden high-pitched laugh.

"Come on," said Spiller, slipping past her, and making toward the door.

Arrietty never forgot her first sight of that upstairs room: the warmth, the sudden cleanliness, the winking candlelight and the smell of home-cooked food.

And so many voices . . . so many people . . .

Gradually, in a dazed way, she began to sort them out, that must be Aunt Lupy embracing her mother—Aunt Lupy so round and glowing, her mother so smudged and lean. Why did they cling and weep, she wondered, and squeeze each other's hands? They had never liked each other—all the world knew that. Homily had thought Lupy stuck-up because, back in the big house, Lupy had lived in the drawing room and (she had heard it rumored) changed for dinner at night. And Lupy despised Homily for living under the kitchen and for pronouncing parquet—"Parkett."

And here was Uncle Hendreary, his beard grown thinner, telling her father that this could not be Arrietty and her father, with pride, telling Uncle Hendreary it could. Those must be the three boy cousins—whose names she had not caught—graduated in size but as like as peas in a pod. And this thin, tall, fairylike creature, neither old nor young, who hovered shyly in the background with a faint uneasy smile, who was she?

Homily screamed when she saw her and clapped her hand to her mouth. "It can't be Eggletina!"

It evidently could. Arrietty stared, too, wondering if she had heard aright: Eggletina, that long-lost cousin who one fine day escaped from under the floor and was never seen again? A kind of legend she had been to Arrietty and a lifelong cautionary tale. Well, here she was, safe and sound, unless they all were dreaming.

And well they might be.

There was something strangely unreal about this room—furnished with doll's house furniture of every shape and size, none of it matching or in proportion. There were chairs upholstered in rep or velvet, some of them too small to sit in and some too steep and large; there were chiffoniers which were too tall and occasional tables far too low; and a toy fireplace with color plaster coals and its fire irons stuck down all-of-a-piece with the fender; there were two make-believe windows with curved pelmets and red satin curtains, each hand-painted with an imitation view—one looked out on a Swiss mountain scene, the other a Highland glen (Eggletina did them, Aunt Lupy boasted in her rich society voice. "We're going

to have a third when we get the curtains—a view of Lake Como from Monte S. Primo"); there were table lamps and standard lamps, flounced, festooned and tasseled, but the light in the room, Arrietty noticed, came from the humble, familiar dips like those they had made at home.

Everybody looked extraordinarily clean and Arrietty became even shyer: she threw a quick glance at her father and mother and was not reassured: none of their clothes had been washed for weeks nor, for some days, had their hands and faces. Pod's trousers had a tear in one knee and Homily's hair hung down in snakes. And here was Aunt Lupy, plump and polite, begging Homily please to take off her things, in the kind of voice, Arrietty imagined, usually reserved for feather boas, opera cloaks and freshly cleaned white kid gloves.

But Homily, who back at home had so dreaded being "caught out" in a soiled apron, knew one worth two of that. She had, Pod and Arrietty noticed with pride, adopted her woman-tried-beyond-endurance role backed up by one called yes-I've-suffered-but-don't-let's-speak-of-it-now; she had invented a new smile, wan but brave, and had—in the same good cause—plucked the two last hairpins out of her dust-filled hair. "Poor dear Lupy," she was saying, glancing wearily about, "what a lot of furniture!

Whoever helps you with the dusting?" And swaying a little, she sank on a chair.

They rushed to support her, as she hoped they might. Water was brought and they bathed her face and hands. Hendreary stood with the tears in his brotherly eyes. "Poor valiant soul," he muttered, shaking his head. "Your mind kind of reels when you think of what she's been through. . . ."

Then, after quick wash and brush-up all round and a brisk bit of eye-wiping, they all sat down to supper. This they ate in the kitchen which was rather a come-down except that, in here, the fire was real: a splendid cooking range made of a large, black door-lock; they poked the fire through the keyhole, which glowed handsomely, and the smoke, they were told, went out through a series of pipes to the cottage chimney behind.

The long, white table was richly spread: it was an eighteenth-century finger-plate off some old drawing-room door—white-enameled and painted with forget-me-nots, supported firmly on four stout pencil stubs where once the screws had been; the points of the pencils emerged slightly through the top of the table; one was copying ink and they were warned not to touch it in case it stained their hands.

There was every kind of dish and preserve— both real and false; pies, puddings, and bottled fruits out of season—all cooked by Lupy—and an imitation leg of mutton and a desk of plaster tarts borrowed from the dolls' house. There were three real tumblers as well as acorn cups and a couple of green glass decanters.

Talk, talk, talk . . . Arrietty, listening, felt dazed. She saw, now, why they had been expected. Spiller, she gathered, having found the alcove bootless and its inmates flown, had salvaged their few possessions and had run and told young Tom. Lupy felt a little faint suddenly when they mentioned this person by name and had to leave the table. She sat awhile in the next room on a frail gilt chair placed just inside the doorway—"between drafts" as she put it—fanning her round red face with a lark's feather.

"Mother's like this about humans," explained the eldest cousin. "It's no good telling her he's tame as anything and wouldn't hurt a fly!"

"You never know," said Lupy darkly, from her seat in the doorway. "He's nearly full grown! And that, they say, is when they start to be dangerous. . . ."

"Lupy's right," agreed Pod. "I'd never trust 'em meself."

"Oh, how can you say that?" cried Arrietty. "Look at the way he snatched us up right out of the jaws of death!"

"Snatched you up?" screamed Lupy from the next room. "You mean—WITH HIS HANDS?"

Homily gave her brave little laugh, listlessly chasing a globule of raspberry around her too slippery plate. "Naturally . . ." She shrugged. "It was nothing, really."

"Oh dear . . ." stammered Lupy faintly. "Oh, you poor thing . . . imagine it! I think," she went on, "if you'll excuse me a moment, I'll just go and lie down . . ." And she heaved her weight off the tiny chair, which rocked as she left it.

"Where did you get all this furniture, Hendreary?" asked Homily, recovering suddenly now that Lupy had gone.

"It was delivered," her brother told her, "in a plain white pillowcase. Someone from the big house brought it down."

"From our house?" asked Pod.

"Stands to reason," said Hendreary. "It's all stuff from that doll's house, remember, they had upstairs in the schoolroom. Top shelf of the toy cupboard, on the right hand side of the door."

"Naturally I remember," said Homily, "seeing that some of it's mine. Pity," she remarked aside to Arrietty, "that we didn't keep that inventory"—she lowered her voice—"the one you made on blotting paper, remember?"

Arrietty nodded: there were going to be fireworks later—she could see that. She felt very tired suddenly; there seemed too much talk and the crowded room felt hot.

"Who brought it down?" Pod was asking in a surprised voice. "Some kind of human being?"

"We reckon so," agreed Hendreary. "It was lying there t'other side of the bank—soon after we got turned out of the badger's set and had set up house in the stove. . . ."

"What stove was that?" asked Pod. "Not the one by the camping site?"

"That's right," Hendreary told him. "Two years we lived there, off and on."

"A bit too close to the Gypsies for my liking," said Pod. He cut himself a generous slice of hot boiled chestnut and spread it thickly with butter.

"You got to be close," Hendreary explained, "like it or not, when you got to borrow."

Pod, about to bite, withdrew the chestnut: he seemed amazed. "You borrowed from caravans?" he exclaimed. "At your age!"

Hendreary shrugged slightly and was modestly silent.

"Well, I never," said Homily admiringly. "There's a brother for you! You think what that means, Pod—"

"I am thinking," said Pod. He raised his head. "What did you do about smoke?"

"You don't have none," Hendreary told him, "not when you cook on gas."

"On gas!" exclaimed Homily.

"That's right. We borrowed a bit o' gas from the gas company: they got a pipe laid all along that bank. The stove was resting on its back, like, you remember? We dug down behind through a flue—a good six weeks we spent in that tunnel. Worth it in the end, though: three pinhole burners we had down there."

"How did you turn 'em on and off?" asked Pod.

"We didn't—once lit, we never let them out. Still burning they are to this day."

"You mean that you still go back there?"

Hendreary, yawning slightly, shook his head (they had eaten well and the room felt very close). "Spiller lives there," he said.

"Oh," exclaimed Homily, "so that's how Spiller cooked! So that's what those bones were! He might have told us," she went on, looking about in a hurt way, "or, at any rate, asked us in—"

"He wouldn't do that," said Hendreary, "once bitten, twice shy, as you might say."

"How do you mean?" asked Homily.

"After we left the badger's set—" began Hendreary and broke off—slightly shamefaced, he seemed, in spite of his smile. "Well, that stove was one of his places: he asked us in for a bite and a sup and we stayed a couple o' years. . . ."

"Once you'd struck gas, you mean," said Pod.

"That's right," said Hendreary. "We cooked and Spiller borrowed."

"Ah—" said Pod. "Spiller borrowed? Now I understand. . . . You and me, Hendreary, we got to face up to it—we're not as young as we was. Not by a long chalk."

"Where is Spiller now?" asked Arrietty suddenly.

"Oh, he's gone off," said Hendreary vaguely; he seemed a little embarrassed and sat there frowning and tapping the table with a pewter spoon (one of a set of six, Homily remembered angrily: she wondered how many were left).

"Gone off where?" asked Arrietty.

"Home, I reckon," Hendreary told her.

"But we haven't thanked him," cried Arrietty. "Spiller saved our lives!"

Hendreary threw off his gloom. "Have a drop of blackberry cordial," he suggested suddenly to Pod. "Lupy's own make. Cheer us all up. . . ."

"Not for me," said Homily firmly, before Pod

could speak. "No good never comes of it as we've found out to our cost."

"But what will Spiller think," persisted Arrietty, and there were tears in her eyes. "We haven't even thanked him?"

Hendreary looked at her, surprised. "Spiller? He don't hold with thanks. He's all right . . ." and he patted Arrietty's arm.

"Why didn't he stay for supper?"

"He don't ever," Hendreary told her. "Doesn't like company. He'll cook something on his own."

"Where?"

"In his stove."

"But that's miles away!"

"Not for Spiller—he's used to it. Goes part way by water."

"And it must be getting dark," Arrietty went on unhappily.

"Now don't you fret about Spiller," her uncle told her. "You eat up your pie. . . ."

Arrietty looked down at her plate (pink celluloid, it was, part of a tea service which she seemed to remember): somehow she had no appetite. She raised her eyes. "And when will he be back?" she asked anxiously.

"He don't come back much. Once a year for his

new clothes. Or if young Tom sends 'im special."

Arrietty looked thoughtful. "He must be lonely," she ventured at last.

"Spiller? No . . . I wouldn't say he was lonely. Some borrowers is made like that. Solitary. You get 'em now and again." He glanced across the room to where his daughter, having left the table, was sitting alone by the fire. "Eggletina's a bit like that . . . Pity, but you can't do nothing about it. Them's the ones as gets this craze for humans—kind of man-eaters, they turns out to be . . ."

When Lupy returned, refreshed from her rest, it all began again: talk, talk, talk . . . and Arrietty slipped unnoticed from the table. But, as she wandered away toward the other room, she heard it going on: talk about living arrangements, about the construction of a suite of rooms upstairs; about what pitfalls there were in this new way of life and the rules they had made to avoid such pitfalls—how you always drew the ladder up last thing at night but that it should never be moved while the men were out borrowing; that the young boys went out as learners, each in turn, but that, true to borrowing tradition, the women would stay at home. She heard her mother declining the use of the kitchen. "Thank you, Lupy," Homily was saying, "it's very kind of you but we'd better begin as we mean to go on, don't you think, quite separate."

And so it starts again, thought Arrietty, as entering the next room she seated herself in a stiff armchair. But no longer quite under the floor—up a little, they would be now, among the lath and plaster: there would be ladders instead of dusty passages and that platform, she hoped, might do instead of her grating.

She glanced about her at the overfurnished room: the doll's house leftovers suddenly looked silly— everything for show and nothing much for use; the false coals in the fireplace looked worn as though scrubbed too often by Lupy and the painted views in the windows had fingermarks round the edge.

She wandered out to the dim-lit platform; this, with its dust and shadows—had she known of such things—was something like going backstage. The ladder was in place, she noticed—a sign that someone was out—but in this case, not so much "out" as "gone." Poor Spiller . . . solitary, they had called him. Perhaps, thought Arrietty self-pityingly, that's what's the matter with me. . . .

There was a faint light, she saw now, in the chasm below her; what at first had seemed a lessening of darkness seemed now a welcoming glow.

Arrietty, her heart beating, took hold of the ladder and set her foot on the first rung. If I don't do it now, she thought desperately, this first evening—perhaps, in the future, I should never dare again; there seemed too many rules in Aunt Lupy's house, too many people, and the rooms seemed too dark and too hot. There may be compensations, she thought—her knees trembling a little as rung after rung she started to climb down—but I'll have to discover them myself.

Soon she stood once again in the dusty entrance hall; she glanced about her and then nervously she looked up; she saw the top of the ladder outlined against the light and the jagged edge of the high platform. It made her feel suddenly dizzy and more than a little afraid: suppose someone, not realizing she was below, decided to pull it up?

The faint light, she realized, came from the hole in the wainscot: the log-box, for some reason, was not laid flush against it—there might well be room to squeeze through. She would like to have one more peep at the room in which, some hours before, young Tom had set them down—to have some little knowledge, however fleeting, of this human dwelling which from now on would compose her world.

All was quiet as she stole toward the gothic-shaped opening. The log-box, she found, was a good inch and a half away. It was easy enough to slip out and ease her tiny body along the narrow passage left between the side of the box and the wall. Again a little frightening: suppose some human being decided suddenly to shove the log-box into place; she would be squashed, she thought, and found long afterward glued to the wainscot, like some strange pressed flower. For this reason, she moved fast, and reaching the box's corner, she stepped out on the hearth.

She glanced about the room. She could see the rafters of the ceiling, the legs of a Windsor chair and the underside of its seat. She saw a lighted candle on a wooden table, and, by its leg, a pile of skins on the floor—ah, this, she realized, was the secret of Spiller's wardrobe.

Another kind of fur lay on the table, just beyond the candle, above a piece of cloth—tawny yellow and somehow rougher. As she stared it seemed to stir. A cat? A fox? Arrietty froze to stillness but she bravely stood her ground. Now the movement became unmistakable: a roll over and a sudden lifting up.

Arrietty gasped—a tiny sound but it was heard.

A face looked back at her, candle-lit and drowsed with sleep, below its thatch of hair. There was a long silence. At last, the boy's lips curved softly into a smile—and very young, he looked, after sleeping, very harmless. The arm on which he had rested his head lay loosely on the table and Arrietty, from where she stood, had seen his fingers relax. A clock was ticking somewhere above her head; the candle flame rose, still and steady, lighting the peaceful room; the coals gave a gentle shudder and settled in the grate.

"Hallo," said Arrietty.

"Hallo," replied young Tom.

Turn the page to discover more exciting books in the Odyssey series.

Other books in the Odyssey series:

L. M. Boston
- ☐ THE CHILDREN OF GREEN KNOWE
- ☐ TREASURE OF GREEN KNOWE
- ☐ THE RIVER AT GREEN KNOWE
- ☐ A STRANGER AT GREEN KNOWE
- ☐ AN ENEMY AT GREEN KNOWE

Mary Norton
- ☐ BED-KNOB AND BROOMSTICK
- ☐ THE BORROWERS
- ☐ THE BORROWERS AFIELD
- ☐ THE BORROWERS AFLOAT

Virginia Hamilton
- ☐ A WHITE ROMANCE
- ☐ JUSTICE AND HER BROTHERS
- ☐ DUSTLAND
- ☐ THE GATHERING

Edward Eager
- ☐ HALF MAGIC
- ☐ KNIGHT'S CASTLE
- ☐ MAGIC BY THE LAKE
- ☐ MAGIC OR NOT?
- ☐ SEVEN-DAY MAGIC
- ☐ THE TIME GARDEN
- ☐ THE WELL-WISHERS

Henry Winterfeld
- ☐ DETECTIVES IN TOGAS
- ☐ MYSTERY OF THE ROMAN RANSOM

Carl Sandburg
- ☐ ROOTABAGA STORIES, PART ONE
- ☐ ROOTABAGA STORIES, PART TWO

Look for these titles and others in the Odyssey series in your local bookstore. To order directly from Harcourt Brace, call Customer Service toll-free at 1-800-543-1918.